I am Z(arah)

a novel
by Kate W. Shea

DEDICATION

For you. Thank you for reading.

CHAPTER 1

"Graham crackers," Zarah cursed as the stoplight in front of her turned red. She eased her Volvo to a halt with exactly seventeen more minutes to catch Rob Eager—her favorite comic book writer since she was a teenager—signing his 100th issue of *The Indomitable X*. Meanwhile, people with skateboards and strollers flooded the suburban downtown crosswalk in front of her car. Yes, it was 68 degrees in Lark Springs, Colorado, but that didn't mean everyone needed to be meandering around Main Street on a Tuesday night.

Green light. Fifteen minutes. Three more blocks. *Please let there be street parking.*

Zarah's hands sweated as she passed parked car after parked car in front of the flat-roofed brick buildings lining Main Street—shops, pubs, restaurants, all with two or three stories of apartments or office space above.

Most people loved that Lark Springs was finally thawing out, now that it was May. Snow still capped the Rocky Mountains in the west, while the aspens budded and the grass hinted of green instead of dead brown. "Don't you just love this weather?" complete strangers would ask each other, responding with nods.

Absurd.

To Zarah, the May thaw meant crowds. A usually solitary walk to get last-minute groceries would now involve *people* for the next four months. She hadn't always hated crowds—she once lived in downtown DC, of all places. But she was different now. And instead of returning a stranger's weather-induced glee with a knowing nod, she now choked on her words and longed to run home and hide in bed alone.

It wasn't their fault. But still—

"There!" Zarah said as she pulled into an open spot directly in front of Comics Inked. She'd driven by the building hundreds of times since it had opened last year, admiring the professional graffiti art on the storefront, imagining the crisp smell of paper and newsprint awaiting her inside.

Ten minutes.

Hundreds of times she'd driven by, but she'd never actually gone inside. In fact, she'd pointedly avoided going inside any building except her apartment and work for the past two years.

She ran her hand over the sleeved 100th issue of *The Indomitable X* in her lap. Closing her eyes and taking a deep breath, she visualized the moment she would meet Rob Eager. He'd greet her with a warm smile, swirl his loopy autograph onto her comic book in thick purple marker, and thank her for being a forever fan. She'd read the first issue eight years ago, and every month since, she'd hungrily flipped the pages of *The Indomitable X*, anticipating the next issue before she even closed the cover. X, an alien made of pure light, had squelched evil and inspired her through high school, through college…and through everything after. And now that she'd barely spoken to anyone, even her father, in two years, X was all she had.

Well, she had Z, too. But Z was different.

Zarah opened her eyes. The sunset stained the Rocky Mountains rose and orange, and families scuttled home after their spur-of-the-moment dinners and shopping downtown.

A little girl in an over-sized Broncos hat, about seven years old, stood in front of Comics Inked next to a cardboard cutout of the Indomitable X, balancing a stack of comics in her arms. That meant there was a line inside for the signing.

Nine minutes.

People were inside.

Zarah's breath became quick and shallow, as if the oxygen in the car was thinning out. Hadn't she thought of this before? Had she thought Rob Eager would be in there all alone, waiting for her? Her stomach twisted into knots at the thought of leaving the sanctuary of her car for a group of strangers nudging each other inside a tight downtown shop. Breathing in each other's air. Talking amongst themselves. Talking to her.

But Rob Eager is just steps away. I can meet him. It's what I've always wanted.

Some sort of pressure, like gravity, pushed on her face, her hands, every part of her body, seeming to glue her to her seat.

I need to stay in the car. I need to stay here where it's safe. I can't be around people.

But Z can, a tiny voice inside her said.

No. Z was just for work, and maybe the grocery store if the delivery service couldn't make it. Z was just for emergencies. This wasn't an emergency.

But it's Rob Eager.

Why couldn't he have done this signing when she was 16? Or 20? Or even the first part of 22? Why now, when she was 24 and broken, when she needed comic books mailed to her, when she couldn't simply get out of her car and walk inside a building full of strangers?

She gasped for air as an unseen force pushed on her body, her heart, her throat—almost strangling her.

Zarah closed her eyes. *Be brave,* she told herself. She

pulled on a gold necklace that had been tucked under her shirt and rubbed its pendant between her thumb and forefinger. As she concentrated on deepening her breaths to long and steady, oxygen filled her lungs and swept through her blood vessels, bringing clarity to her thoughts and melting the glue holding her to her seat.

Be like Z.

Zarah opened her eyes and looked into her rear-view mirror, where she watched her frizzy red hair coil into ringlets of its own accord. Her freckles faded, and her pale white skin began to glow like stardust. Her blouse and skirt transformed into a yellow long-sleeved dress with a red-orange Z across her chest, and a matching mask framed her near-black eyes.

She grasped the door handle and stepped out of her car on stilettos.

Zarah no longer existed. That frizzy-haired, terrified file clerk had fallen away like an invisibility cloak to reveal Z.

"It's you! It's Z!" cried the little girl in front of the store as she bounced up and down on her toes, dropping her stack of comics in excitement. She pushed back her hat to uncover big brown eyes. "You're my favorite superhero!"

Z's heart swelled. She'd come to see her famous friend, the Indomitable X, and his biographer, Rob, but to this little girl, she was the greater hero. Z's hair draped over her thin shoulders as she knelt down to the seven-year-old's level, below the heads of a gathering crowd. "What's your name?" she asked the girl.

"Tazmeen." The girl grinned, her tongue showing through missing front teeth.

"Tazmeen," Z repeated, standing. A crowd had already formed around her, phones raised for pictures and videos. Z's heart raced. "Let me show you something, Tazmeen."

Z ran her fingers through her delicate ringlets, pulling on the static, straightening her hair to silky smooth all the way to the ends. She tightened her fists to contain the energy as it tried to burst from her fingers. Then, with a harpy cry, she thrust her fists in the air and opened them toward the sunset, where lightning flashed against the backdrop of the Rocky Mountains.

Loud cheers erupted from the crowd. Z lowered her arms and grinned at her fans, feeling their adoration wrap around her heart. On the planet Marathon, she'd been buried for her fiery hair. Cursed and left for dead. But these humans celebrated her for who she was.

After taking one last look at Tazmeen, whose brown eyes sparked with awe, Z blew the crowd a kiss and turned toward her friend, the Indomitable X.

X was unmistakable: a human-shaped silhouette of yellow light, save for the two dark sunspots of his eyes, leaning against the front of the building. Had Z not been raised on a sun planet, she would have needed to shield her eyes.

"My dearest Z!" he boomed as he threw out his thick, muscular arms.

Z gingerly stepped into his embrace, her thin fingers scarcely reaching his back. Her cheek pressed against his, and the warmth filled her with thoughts of a real home, like the ones in Earth's children's books where parents hugged their kids before bed.

"Favorite superhero'? You've gotten popular these last two years," he said as he released her.

Behind her, the people on the crowded sidewalks of downtown Lark Springs still shouted and waved. Cars stopped in traffic while their drivers stepped out and snapped pictures. Main Street glittered like stars.

"They love you, Z," X said.

"They love you more."

He chuckled. "You've always underestimated yourself." His eyes locked onto hers. "Thank you, dear, for coming to Rob's signing. I know you've never loved all this pomp and circumstance."

Z looked back at Tazmeen's wide, gap-toothed grin. "Perhaps it's growing on me. Besides, I wouldn't miss the 100th issue of your biography."

"I thought we were past flattery," he said, rolling his eyes. "Why don't you come inside and meet Rob?"

Zarah blinked at the cardboard cutout of the Indomitable X leaning against the entrance to Comics

Inked. The girl had gone inside, and Zarah was still parked in her Volvo.

Five minutes.

"Come on, Zarah," she said to herself. "Rob Eager is in that building, and you're meeting him before he leaves."

She curled her fingers into fists. *I have to be like Z.*

Closing her eyes, Zarah once more imagined her hair coiling, her skin glimmering, her mask hugging her face. *You've got this, Z.* She pulled the car door handle.

As she opened her eyes and stepped onto Main Street, she clutched her comic book to her chest like armor. Her heel clicked shakily on the sidewalk. *You're doing it. You're walking on the sidewalk. You're walking toward the building.* Another step.

At the same moment, a young man about her age with hair like Jimi Hendrix with bedhead peeked out of the store's front door. He wore jeans, a Wolverine tee-shirt, and a gray flannel shirt that hung off of his slim body. As he reached for the Indomitable X cutout, he caught Zarah's eyes through his green thick-framed glasses, and a sheepish smile grew on his brown, lightly-freckled face. "Hey."

Zarah's heart thumped in her chest at being noticed. *Be like Z,* she thought. *Say something normal,* she thought, like, *"I'm here to meet Mr. Eager. He's here for another five minutes, right?"* But in reality, she just stood stock-still, staring at the young man.

He stepped toward her. Normally, she'd back away from a stranger. But something about him—his smile— seemed safe.

No. No one is safe. Nothing is safe. You thought that before the police tape. The screams. The gunshots. But you know better now.

She gritted her teeth. *You're doing it again. Stop being crazy. Stop being Zarah. Be Z.* But her breath quickened and the air seemed to thin and her stomach cramped at the thought of the *people* blocking her way to her idol and—

"Mr. Eager's still signing," the young man said as he

pulled the cutout next to him. "Crowd's gone. There's just this little girl inside. Freaking adorable." His face lit up as he smiled and shook his head. "Walking in with her little stack of comics and that big old hat. And—" He cut himself off. "Sorry. I'm rambling. I'm not normally this awkward. Well, actually, I am. I just, you know, hide it."

Her panic paused and she took a long breath in. *Crowd's gone.* Maybe he hated crowds, too. Maybe he was awkward enough to understand.

No one understands.

But he seemed warm and kind and goofy and…she could almost breathe normally. "Me too," she said. "Except I don't hide it very well."

"Well, the comic store's a haven, then, for us weirdos who can't make eye contact or speak in sentences." His eyes widened. "Not that you're a weirdo. I'm a weirdo," he said as he gestured to himself. "What I mean is…I'm Greg. I semi-obviously work here." He held out his hand.

She should take it. The "normal" thing to do was shake his hand.

Three minutes. This was her moment. But the pause in her panic faded as quickly as it had come. What if a last-minute horde came for the signing and what if someone had a gun and what if she could just avoid all of it by just turning around and going home alone where she belonged—in isolation? Tears welled in her eyes and her stomach churned and she couldn't breathe, and if she couldn't shake this man's hand, how could she ask for Rob Eager's autograph?

You can't. You're not Z.

Zarah turned around, slipped inside her car, and turned the key in the ignition.

"Wait!" she thought she heard him call as she pulled away toward home.

CHAPTER 2

Ten minutes later, the summer sunset poured through a single window at the far end of Zarah's 300-square-foot apartment. The grapefruit-tinted glow washed over her polished oak desk and bookcase, crept across the lavender quilt on her bed, climbed up the peeling kitchenette cabinets, and rested at her feet in the doorway.

Usually, the silence of her apartment enveloped her like a warm, soft blanket. But tonight, the quiet tightened around her neck like a noose.

I walked away from Rob Eager.

Coward, a voice inside her said. *Pathetic.*

She pulled on quick breaths of air as limpness crept through her body. Her vision faded, darkening all except the sunset. That light grew brighter, searing her retinas, leaving the impression of the Indomitable X glowing like Helios or Ra. She willed her limbs to move, to walk through the doorway, to lock the door behind her, to take off her heels and her blouse and skirt and change into shorts and a tank top, but her body just tingled with tiny pinpricks.

You can't walk into a comic book store. Can't even walk into your own apartment. You're weak.

She tried to focus on her breath.

You're nothing.

Breathe deeply, slowly.

You gave up on your dreams. Again.

A hamster's squeak broke her thoughts. The glow of the sunset softened, and her vision painted her apartment back around her—bed, desk, bookshelf, Indomitable X posters on red brick walls. She inhaled deeply, returning feeling to her limbs, and touched the doorframe to steady herself.

The hamster's squeaking persisted.

"I'm coming, X," Zarah said to the hamster—named after the Indomitable X, of course—as she closed and latched the door behind her. Hands shaking, she pulled off her heels and stepped barefoot between her kitchen and bathroom, past her bed on the left, to her desk on the far wall. A clothesline ran along the right side of the room as a makeshift closet.

In the middle of her desk, just under the window, sat a cage where a little blue-gray hamster peeked out of his pile of litter, whiskers nearly as long as his body. Zarah pulled out a sunflower seed from a repurposed heart-shaped box of chocolates her dad had sent last Valentine's Day, and slipped it through the bars to X. He yanked the seed out of Zarah's fingers, curled into a ball, and began nibbling.

"See, I couldn't have gone into Comics Inked," she reasoned with the hamster, her body finally settling again. "I had to come home to give you treats."

She set her unsigned 100th issue of *The Indomitable X* next to the hamster's cage, the book's lack of autograph a vibrant manifestation of her failings. On the front, the Indomitable X glowed like the sun above the DC skyline: the pillars of the Lincoln Memorial, the tall point of the Washington Monument, and the dome of the Capitol, a throwback to Rob Eager's first issue.

Two years ago, she'd lived in DC for an internship at the Smithsonian's Museum of Ancient History, and she'd settled into an apartment alive with the voices of three roommates, the smell of onions and peppers as they cooked vegan tacos, the steady beat of global pop music. The first night, she and her roommates had crept up to the roof with a box of wine. In the sticky sauna of that DC summer night, the hum of cars and helicopters masking the songs of crickets and cicadas, she'd marveled at the glittering lights of that same skyline, her new home, the Indomitable X's home.

She couldn't have stayed in DC, of course. Not after what happened. Now she longed for the Zarah on that roof, the Zarah who brought out her guitar that night to play ambient chords to suit the mood, then wrote songs about the skyline after a few glasses of wine. She longed for the Zarah who would have walked into the closest comic book store with her roommates—even though they didn't like comics—and taken pictures with Rob Eager and posted them online. Or for the Zarah who went to college at Boulder, hair swept back into a handkerchief and guitar slung across her back. Or even high school Zarah, who was president of the comic book club.

But that Zarah—those Zarahs—were dead.

After leaving her internship, she'd moved in with her dad in Montana, where he was chasing his lifelong dream of playing the fiddle on his front porch in full view of the mountains. She'd stayed for two months, until one day, wholly unannounced, he gave her an ultimatum over a dinner of black bean stew. "You can live here as long as you'd like," he said as steam rose from the soup and wove through his graying red beard. "If you'd just see a doctor, Zaralah."

A doctor. He'd meant a therapist. But a therapist couldn't change what had happened. And if her dad couldn't deal with the new her—well, then she'd just leave. She didn't need anyone but Z. No one else understood.

No one else could.

In the end, her father had settled for giving her X the

hamster along with space and silence, save for a monthly postcard and issue of *The Indomitable X.*

All of which brought her here to Lark Springs, where she'd grown up. Zarah pulled her eyes away from the comic, then peered over X's cage and out her top fifth-story window onto Main Street. The old brick building provided her an off-street parking spot, an alleyway stairwell, and the near-certainty that she'd never need to set foot on the crowded sidewalk of Main Street Lark Springs. On the first floor stood an abandoned sushi buffet, whose boarded windows drew only the occasional street musician playing "Stairway to Heaven," "Brown Eyed Girl," or "Wonderwall" in the evenings, though presently all was silent. Gazing three blocks west toward the Rocky Mountains and Pike's Peak, Zarah wondered if Rob Eager had already left for Denver.

"Why don't you come inside and meet Rob?" asked the Indomitable X, linking arms with Z.

"But I'm late," said Z. "Shouldn't you both be on your way north?"

The Indomitable X laughed and gestured to the crowd behind them, still snapping pictures. "Oh, Z, being late doesn't count when you've stopped to greet your fans. That's one of the top rules of superherodom." He opened the door to Comics Inked and released her arm. "After you."

Inside Comics Inked, origami buildings rose like skyscrapers, and the pathways between them glistened gold, set with medals and city keys won by the superheroes inside. Rob Eager leaned over a table made of game boards: Settlers of Catan, Chutes and Ladders, Trivial Pursuit. A mop of salt-and-pepper hair covered his eyes as he signed Tazmeen's comic book.

Tazmeen smiled at Rob and skipped away, leaving only Z and X in line.

Z's heart swelled. Finally, she'd meet this man who had so lovingly detailed X's life, from his birth as a solar flare to his descent onto Earth to his days battling Dr. Nemesinister to repeatedly saving the Capitol. "This is my dear friend, Z," said X as Z approached Rob.

As Rob Eager stood, his mop fell away from his face to reveal ice-blue eyes. He smiled at Z—just like in his headshot—and extended his hand.

Crack!

A car backfired outside Zarah's window.

She screamed and leapt back from her desk. Frantically, she wheeled her gaze to each corner of the room. It sounded like the crack of a shotgun, and she knew it wasn't, but she was there again and

Crack!-Crack!-Crack!

The sudden noise pierced Comics Inked, and its origami towers and glittering paths fell away to reveal stone tablets and broken bits of jewelry on dimly-lit closet shelves. Zarah breathed in the musty smell of the museum's Mesopotamia storage closet.

High-pitched, blood-curdling screams erupted outside the door. Indistinct shouting. Pounding feet. Shattering glass.

The doorknob convulsed.

She dove behind a pile of tablets. Shivering, she curled into the fetal position and tried to breathe, but her lungs were paralyzed.

Crack!-Crack!-Crack!

X squeaked and pawed at his cage.

Zarah blinked. The golden glow of the evening sun rested like dust across the floor of her apartment. She wasn't in the museum's closet. That closet was on the other side of the country.

It's over, she reminded herself, breathing deeply. *It's over. It's over. That was two years ago.* Zarah rubbed her temples and sat down on her bed. She reached for Bunny the stuffed koala, who sat perched on a pillow, and clung to him.

CHAPTER 3

```
"spaghetti noodle"
```

The phrase jumped out at Zarah as she scanned an office visit report the next day. Technically, she wasn't supposed to be reading the patients' reports, but she always told Franklin the nurse that she'd break just about any rule, short of growing pot in the window, to make filing medical papers more interesting. And after last night, the prospect of growing and ingesting a perfectly-legal but office-rule-breaking plant seemed comparable to ambrosia.

```
The patient complained of
feeling a "spaghetti noodle"
sensation in his legs.
```

Well, that wasn't as exciting as she'd hoped. In her mind, what happened was:

```
The patient's brain suddenly
turned into spaghetti noodles
```

```
and spilled out of his ears,
right in the middle of the exam
room. Like a big octopus king,
he wrapped his spaghetti brain
tentacles around Dr. Desai and
Franklin. Z burst from the file
room and sprinted toward their
cries, her fists tremoring with
primed lightning.
```

But, instead, the patient was just boring old Bob Stedford who complained of pasta-themed symptoms and visited at least once a week. Zarah continued through her pile with the resigned futility of Sisyphus. Grab the paper. Grab the file. Open the prongs. Shove in the paper. Close the prongs.

For the better part of nine years, this had been her routine—in the summers during school and full-time for the past two years. With each file shut, another minute ticked by in the back room of Dr. Desai's cardiology practice, home to towering shelves of files, a countertop, and the occasional visit from Franklin.

She had thought she'd found her break two years ago at the museum. Then the police tape, the shutdown, the news. Now, job postings with words like "interpersonal skills," "verbal communication," and the dreaded "team environment" struck her with the same terror that *The Exorcist* had caused her when she was five. So she'd asked her boss Kris if she could return here and go back to filing papers. It was safe here. Paper didn't ask questions.

Franklin, a stocky Black man in his 40s, strode in from the hallway, wearing dinosaur scrubs and carrying a file. With a unibrow reminiscent of Oscar the Grouch and a laugh like Eddie Murphy's, he was the only person who made Zarah feel, well, normal. When he'd first started working at the office last year, he told Zarah she was too skinny and brought her shrimp lo mein from Chinese Palace. He never asked her about her past or her family or school or the dreaded what-the-hell-are-you-going-to-do-with-your-life question, like most people did. Maybe it was because he didn't know her before the internship, or maybe he just liked quiet recluses. Zarah only knew it was a relief that she could go weeks without seeing anyone in the office but Franklin.

"So tell me something, Zarah," he said, his voice gruff like the scratch of an old record.

"I ate a banana for breakfast," she said, reaching for the file he was holding.

He held the folder close, like he was withholding a treat from a dog. "You know that's not the something I want to know. The signing last night—how did it go?"

"I..." she sputtered and looked down at the countertop.

"Damn! You chickened out?" said Franklin, punching her playfully in the shoulder.

Embarrassment singed her cheeks. She kept her face down, trying to focus on the specks of color running through the Formica countertop. She'd been so distracted by Bob Stedford and his spaghetti brain, she'd almost forgotten about last night's debacle.

"I should've offered to go with you," said Franklin, his voice softening. "I know that weird glowing alien is your hero."

"It's fine." She looked up. His usual smirk had faded into a straight, serious mouth, and the lines on his forehead had softened. "Let's look at that file," Zarah said, reaching for it again.

"He's gone up to Denver, right? What if I drove you after work?"

And run away crying like I did last night, then have to ride two hours home with you in shamed silence? No thank you. "Franklin, the file. Please."

"All right, all right," he said as he handed it to her.

She opened the crisp, thin manila folder—a new

patient. A few months ago, Franklin had stopped chiding Zarah for reading the patient's charts like they were "trashy romance novels" and had started singling out one file a day to discuss. Sometimes he'd even have her shadow him with a patient. Interaction with a patient, of course, required her to become Z, but the occasional transformation was manageable. Zarah had no designs on going to nursing school, but at least these chats with Franklin made the day feel less like purgatory.

"Symptoms?" she asked.

"Palpitations and syncope." *Racing heart and fainting*, Zarah knew the symptoms to mean. "He's young, though—26," Franklin added as she scanned the solitary page of hospital notes.

```
        syncope


                      normal EKG

        SOB

                           no children

        dizziness

           Gilgamesh
```

Zarah raised an eyebrow and looked closer at the name.

```
        Last Name: Normand

        First Name: Gregory

        Middle Name: Gilgamesh
```

Memories flashed in Zarah's mind from the museum:

Mesopotamian tablets, jars, bowls, ceramic reliefs, and cuneiform texts of *The Epic of Gilgamesh*—an ancient demigod and king depicted with broad shoulders, a beard down to his chest, and a lion in his arms. She imagined the letters on the report in front of her scattering and reorganizing into a more exciting story:

> The Great Gilgamesh's long,
> curled black hair draped over
> his bare brown back like a cape,
> and a sheepskin skirt covered
> the lower half of his body. A
> round emerald and gold amulet
> nestled between the muscles on
> his chest. His eyes regarded Dr.
> Desai with curiosity under thick
> furrowed brows.
>
> "I cannot save the city if I
> must suffer this illness," the
> Great Gilgamesh said to Dr.
> Desai.
>
> "I thought superheroes couldn't
> get sick," said the doctor,
> pressing her stethoscope just
> above the amulet.
>
> "Do you know nothing?" growled
> the Great Gilgamesh. "We are not
> gods. Seven days and nights I
> sat beside the body of my
> friend, Enkidu, mourning him.
> Must I die now, too?"

"Thoughts?" asked Franklin.

Zarah's mind returned to the patient's symptoms. "Everything was normal at the hospital. We can't know what's wrong until we run some more tests."

Franklin nodded. "Such as?"

She considered the question. They'd start with an EKG—short for electrocardiogram—a spikey line graph of the heart's electrical activity that Franklin performed on every patient. Even though the patient's EKG had been normal in the hospital, it could change during "episodes," times when his heart was racing or he felt dizzy. Then a stress test would show how running on a treadmill affected his heart.

Zarah gave Franklin her suggestions, and he nodded. "Good, good. Now come with me to Exam Room 5. Bring the file."

"Can't you carry it yourself?"

"Of course I can. But you're running the EKG."

"What?" The floor felt like it had dropped out from under her.

"I've been telling you for months: when I finally convince Kris and Dr. Desai to go digital, I don't want you to be unemployed. You're smart, and you don't need to be a registered nurse to help me out." He grabbed a pen and blank office visit form from Zarah's counter, stuffed them into the file, and handed it to her.

"No, Franklin, really," she protested as he grabbed her shoulders and guided her like a shopping cart out of her filing area and down the narrow wallpapered hall. Her heart raced. She'd shadowed Franklin before, but never actually run the test. She needed time, needed calm to become Z.

"Couldn't I practice with you first?" she pleaded.

Franklin stopped and knocked a friendly beat on a wooden door with a golden "5" sticker. "And have you see me shirtless? Good God, Zarah. I'm not that cruel." Before Zarah could object further, he opened the door.

"Hello, Mr. Normand!" he boomed.

Zarah lingered in the doorway as Franklin introduced himself and pulled on blue nitrile gloves. Around Franklin's large frame, Zarah could only see the patient's dangling feet from where he sat on the exam table. He was wearing stained, fraying sandals that would have made Jesus' disciples look fashionable.

The image of the Great Gilgamesh in Zarah's mind began to fade. Not that she'd actually expected an ancient Babylonian demigod to be seeing a cardiologist in Lark Springs, but it would at least have been exciting.

"This is Zarah," Franklin said, motioning for her to step into the room. "She's in training. Do you mind if she assists me today?"

She pulled on gloves from a box hanging on the wall and stepped past Franklin into the exam room.

The slender young man sitting shirtless on the exam table, hands tucked between his knees, stared wide-eyed back at Zarah through rectangular green-framed glasses. Clumps of hair grew in irregular tufts from his chest, in contrast with a thick, tousled halo of black hair on his head. Even though his skin was naturally light brown with dark freckles, he still seemed sickly pale. "I don't mind at all," he said, eyebrow raised as he scrutinized her.

The clerk from Comics Inked.

Zarah looked at her feet and let her curls cover her face as Franklin took the patient's blood pressure and pulse. *Marathon in the heavens,* Zarah silently prayed to Z's god as Franklin chatted with the patient, *please don't let him recognize me as the girl who cried and ran away when he tried to shake my hand.*

"Pulse: 70. Blood pressure: 110/70," Franklin called out the patient's vitals, and Zarah wrote them in his chart, eyes glued firmly to the paper. "Looks good, Mr. Normand. What brings you in today?"

"I've been…I don't know." He hesitated.

Zarah looked up. Gregory Gilgamesh Normand was

staring at his knees. His face was scrunched in a way that he was either about to throw up or willing himself to become invisible. *I know that grimace*, she thought. *He wishes he was Z too. Or the Great Gilgamesh. Or someone, just not himself.*

"Sometimes I'm dizzy," he said. "I passed out at work once, so my boss took me to the hospital." He chuckled, eyes still downcast. "Carried me, actually. Didn't trust the ambulance to come fast enough. He's an odd one."

"No kidding," Zarah whispered, surprised by the sound of her own voice. The hospital was nearly a mile from Comics Inked.

The patient glanced at Zarah and smiled. *Graham crackers*, that smile made her feel like she'd curled up in a warm bed of fluffy blankets away from the rest of the world. It was stupid, she knew. He was a stranger.

A blush crept across her cheeks. *Why had she said anything?*

"It was just the one time, though," he said as he stared back at his knees. "I don't think I need a bunch of tests."

"Today's test is standard," said Franklin. "We perform an electrocardiogram every visit." As he explained how an EKG worked, Mr. Normand nodding silently, Zarah retrieved alcohol wipes from a supply cabinet in the corner.

"—and then Zarah will place the electrode stickers on your wrists, ankles, and here along your ribs—"

Marathon's ass. She'd forgotten that Franklin meant for her to do the entire test herself. Well, that wasn't going to happen. No matter how badly Franklin wanted her to learn how to do this test, it would have to wait until another time. Maybe it would be easier with a kindly old woman or something. Not this young man who kept smiling at her and making her feel safe in a way that she couldn't handle, in a way that had her frozen in the doorway of her apartment last night because he'd caught her off-guard, broken the spell of Z.

No, Zarah only had room in her life for one work

friend, one hamster, and one monthly postcard from Dad. She had no room for this patient to ask why she'd run away last night and keep asking and asking about her life until she just had to be Z all the time because that was the only way not to seem completely unbalanced.

Hoping Franklin would take the hint, Zarah handed the wipes to him as he finished his EKG monologue.

Franklin pursed his lips and glared at Zarah as if to consider asking a question, but then wiped down the patient's wrists, ankles, and ribs. Then, with a grin, he took the file from her and handed her the electrode stickers.

Nausea tickled at the corners of her mouth as she stared at the electrodes. Each had a color-coded tab, to which they'd clip wires that ran to the EKG printer, like a lie detector test in an old movie. She knew how to apply them. But her hands started to sweat and her breath started to quicken and—

"I recognize you," said the patient.

Heart thumping in her ears, Zarah looked down at the scuffed linoleum floor.

"You were at the signing last night, right?"

Fuck. Questions. Zarah can't answer. Need to be Z. She tried to visualize her hair smoothing and her skin glittering, but the image of Z kept sliding away like oil.

Okay, no Z. Could she lie and say he must be thinking of someone else?

But her hair. She'd always stood out. Always been so recognizable.

"Yes," she capitulated, closing her eyes, "that was me."

"Mr. Eager signed a few extra copies," he said. "You can have one if you want."

What?

She opened her eyes as an imaginary weight fell off of her.

It wasn't really a second chance—after all, Rob Eager was in Denver now—but she suddenly longed for that signed comic book like she usually longed for the quiet of her apartment. "That would be wonderful," she said, meeting his eyes. They were amber with green flecks, like pieces of ancient Egyptian jewelry.

He grinned. "Good, then! Call it a gift for helping keep me alive."

"In the spirit of keeping you alive, Mr. Normand," said Franklin, "lay down on your back, and then let's see your right wrist." Mr. Normand nodded, then silently followed Franklin's instructions. *Yes, back to work.* Zarah stared at the spot where she knew the electrode belonged on the patient's raised wrist. Now that she'd talked to this patient, she really needed to appear sensible. *Graham crackers, he just offered me a signed copy of the 100th issue of my favorite comic of all time.* But if she couldn't be Z…. She looked at the door. Could she run? *No. That would look ridiculous.* The walls started closing in, and the temperature rose like a sauna.

She closed her eyes, breathed deeply, rubbed the pendant she always wore tucked into her shirt, and tried again to become Z.

Zarah is only Z's cover, like Superman's Clark Kent, she told herself. *Zarah is just Z pretending to be shy. Z is an immovable force, sole survivor from her planet. I'm not Zarah.*

Zarah isn't real.

Calm spread through her body like a lapping lake. She peeled back an electrode sticker and placed it on Mr. Normand's left wrist. His skin was cold, like clay, and her hands shook a little as she touched him.

I did it.

No—Z did it.

She continued—to the left wrist, then the ankles, and finally the ribs, which were pressing against his skin—while Franklin helped adjust her hands. "Beautiful!" Franklin said as he turned on the machine and insisted that the patient neither move nor speak.

Click-click-whir.   Click-click-whir.   The machine amplified the silence between the three of them. Mr. Normand stared at the ceiling, and part of Zarah—no, she was being Z right now—part of Z wanted to protect him. She didn't know why; what on earth did he need protecting from? But she knew what it felt like to be scared and alone—wait, who did? Who was she right now? She felt Z begin to pull her fabric away from Zarah's, Z's arms reaching to be free.

No. Stay. Please.

Z knew what it felt like to be scared and alone, buried and left for dead.

But I'm not Z.

Yes! Yes you are!

Zarah knew what it felt like to be scared and alone, too. Hiding in a closet. Screams outside.

Please! Stay!

Click-click-whir.

She focused on Mr. Normand, lying still on the table. He was human too, human like Zarah.

Zarah's shoulders slumped as Z slipped away from her, pulling her lightning bolts, her lifeblood into the ether.

Franklin completed the test, bade the patient farewell, and assured him that Dr. Desai would be there in a few minutes. As Franklin ushered Zarah out of the room, she turned back to Mr. Normand, hoping to catch his eye. But he was making the I'm-going-to-puke-or-disappear face at his knees again.

After he closed the door, Franklin clasped Zarah on the shoulder. "Thought you were going to freeze in there," he said. "But good work. I'm late for my next patient—catch you later."

Zarah nodded and turned back down the hallway toward the file room. She felt drained, as if she'd actually physically transformed into Z. It was early yet, probably about ten o'clock. Could she curl up in a corner behind some files and sleep? Would anyone even notice?

A familiar garumph broke her thoughts, and Zarah looked up to face her office manager standing in the file room doorway. A stout white woman in her 50s, Kris sported her usual cropped gray bob and matching gray pants suit. Frown lines—presumably from decades of eating lemons and hating her life—framed her pale pink lips. She stared at the files on Zarah's countertop. "Your stack of files is out of hand," Kris said in a somehow-sneering monotone. "Falling over. Get them done."

Ah, Kris—or as Zarah liked to call her in her daily debriefing to X the hamster: the Rhinocerkris—ever eloquent. Still, these days, Zarah almost welcomed Kris's barking orders over small talk. *Better to have a boss who never asks questions*, she told herself. And, after all, Kris had given her this job back full-time when she'd needed it.

"Yes, Kris," said Zarah, her hopes of a secret nap disintegrating.

After blinking twice, Kris grunted and walked away.

Unfazed by Kris's lack of verbal response, Zarah entered the file room and returned to her filing, which was, indeed, stacked so high that it was falling over. Grab the paper. Grab the file. Open the prongs. Shove in the paper. Close the prongs. *Don't stop to read. Just get this done.* Grab the paper. Grab the file. Open the prongs—

"Um, Zarah, right?"

She looked up from her one-woman assembly line to see Gregory Gilgamesh Normand standing in the hall, now fully clothed in a Judge Dredd tee-shirt, green flannel shirt, and wide smile.

"Franklin said I could find you here." He shoved his hands in his pockets and rocked back and forth on his heels. "I'm serious about the comic book. We're open 'til seven tonight. You should stop by."

She thought about the comic book back in her apartment, devoid of the autograph it was meant to hold. She summoned what atoms she had left of Z and tightened her fists. Z could do it. Z would go.

Zarah isn't real. She's just a cover.

"I'll be there."

"Awesome!" Mr. Normand waved as he walked away.

CHAPTER 4

The persistent, almost irregular psychedelic soul beat of Orange Coffee Mug's "O Gandalf, My Gandalf" pulsed in Greg Normand's ear buds as he stepped off the bus, its exhaust pipe coughing like an asthmatic smoker. The dusty smell of the bus gave way to the aromas of lamb, honey, and nutmeg.

He inhaled appreciatively before walking up Main Street past the Greek restaurant where 20-somethings ate lunch outside in the temperate summer heat. Along the sidewalk, budding trees stood about eight feet tall and spaced with precision—like a line of leafy Ent Rockettes—wrapped tight with strands of lights.

Ah, suburban life. Sure, these five-story brick buildings were no Houston skyscrapers, but they were a far cry from the trailer parks of Wilford, Texas, where he'd lived until six months ago. A few blocks to the north he could find Lebanese food, a block west was Afghan kabob, and five blocks south was the best Vietnamese pho he'd ever had. Plus, here in Lark Springs, he was no longer the only mixed Black-white kid in town, the kid whose dad packed currywurst or daal soup in his lunch instead of sandwiches or cold pizza, or the nerd who listened to bands his friends had never heard of instead of Lynyrd Skynyrd.

He was just a guy.

Yeah, a guy with a bad heart.

A half hour ago, Dr. Desai had pushed up her thick round glasses and nodded empathetically. "Your doctor in Texas was right, Mr. Normand," she said. "Wolff-Parkinson-White Syndrome is usually harmless. Many people don't even know they have it." Her slight Indian accent sprinkled her words as she sat on a stool to be eye-level with Greg, who sat on the exam table. "It's fortunate you already have your diagnosis. But I still recommend further testing. While your readings today are normal, I'm concerned about your fainting spell."

"That was just one time," Greg protested. "I walk to work. I walked here from the bus stop." He patted his chest. "Heart feels fine now."

But Dr. Desai shook her head. "You have an extra electrical pathway in your heart, like a road that was never meant to be built but that people keep driving on. We might need to stop traffic."

"Stop traffic!' Greg's stomach lurched. "Like stop my heart?"

"Not necessarily. I know this can be scary," she said, putting a hand on Greg's shoulder. "But we are here to take care of you. This is a very treatable disease. We just need to get you in for a stress test as soon as possible."

Sure, that was all reassuring—you know, that bit about stopping his currently-beating heart and everything. But a stress test on a part-time salary at a comic book store? Maybe it was just altitude sickness, or anxiety, or any of the other 50 things the internet linked to fainting. Maybe both doctors were wrong.

In Greg's ear buds, the music changed to the aggressive screamo rock of Anonymous Graffiti, mercifully pushing all heart-related thoughts out of his mind. He reached the concrete stairs of the apartment he shared with his friends Bastian and Fred, just a block from the bus stop. He pushed through the door and trudged up the wide wooden staircase inside the atrium. In its heyday, it had opened on Main Street as Lark Springs Youth Music Conservatory, but after the Great Depression, three fires, and a DEA bust of its staff, it had been remodeled into an apartment building. Or at least, that was what the landlady had said.

As Greg approached the top of the staircase and turned right down the beige-and-blue wallpapered hallway, he wondered what Fred and Bastian would say if he told them he had an actual disease with a name. Bastian would, of course, research all of the doctors in the area and insist on paying for the testing. And Fred, well... Fred had spent most of their acquaintance body-slamming Greg into lockers and calling him a loser, and it wasn't until Bastian beat the living crap out of Fred in eleventh grade that he'd started acting like half a human. So, who knew? Maybe Fred would feel bad. Or maybe he'd just shrug and not give a shit.

Greg unlocked the chipped door and entered their three-bedroom apartment, which smelled of sandalwood and cigarette smoke. After years of not being repainted between residents, the walls were the color of a wet coffee filter and cracked where Greg supposed the support beams were. The yellow linoleum floor had squares and corners missing. A few feet from the door sat a tattered lime-green sofa where Fred and Bastian stared at their 65-inch flatscreen displaying the loading screen for *Band of Soldiers 4*.

"Just in fucking time!" shouted Fred. With beady eyes and a pointed nose like a yellow-white ferret, Fred's saving grace was his thick blonde bun and Viking-style beard. His clean black tee-shirt—rather than the usual food-stained white undershirt—indicated he was bartending tonight.

Bastian, unchanged from the pressed khakis, shirt, and tie he'd worn to work that morning, patted the open seat next to him. In contrast to Fred, Bastian was strong-jawed, brown-skinned, clean-shaven, and smiling. "Sit down and run a mission with us, Greggie. I'm headed back to the office in five."

"I can't, guys," Greg said, closing and locking the door behind him. "I'm just grabbing a bite before work." His stomach lurched. *Work. I forgot. That girl, Zarah. She's coming by.*

"How'd your appointment go?" asked Bastian, holding out a game controller from their tire-and-plywood coffee table.

Greg took the controller and plopped down between his roommates. "My EKG is still normal. So it's probably the altitude or something." *It's not. But I'll be fine. Or maybe I'll be dead tomorrow. Who knows?* An urban desert battlefield materialized on the TV screen in quadrants, and the three of them manned their on-screen guns. "So do you guys remember how I said there was, like, the most stunningly beautiful woman at Comics Inked last night?"

"Yeah, the girl who ran away from you?" said Fred.

"Yes, her. She, uh, ran my EKG today. Like stuck my chest with electrodes." *As if the Universe declared our first meeting not awkward enough.*

"Kinky." Fred pushed loose blond hair out of his face without breaking his on-screen aim. "Oh, powned his ass!" he cried as he knifed his opponent in the face.

Greg tossed a grenade through a window and obliterated a room of enemies.

"Badass," said Fred, shouldering him.

"So," Greg said, "you might remember how you guys said she, like, wasn't real and all this stuff." He ducked behind a stack of crates to recharge his armor. "But she is. And she's coming by the store tonight."

"That's awesome, Greggie," Bastian said as he blew out the windows of a building with a grenade launcher. "Think she's single?"

"Who cares?" said Fred.

"Pay attention, Fred," snapped Bastian. "Sniper, third-floor balcony."

"Already got 'em," said Greg, centering his crosshairs on the sniper's head and pulling the trigger.

"Nice shot," said Bastian. "But I'm the one who works on an Air Force Base with some of the best-looking guys in the country. How are you the first one to get a date?"

"It's not a date. I'm giving her a comic she wanted."

Fred groaned. "You don't even know this girl and you're giving her a gift? Fuck women. They're the worst."

"Fred, shut it! Another fucking sniper," snapped Bastian.

Greg sighed as he peered at the opponent through the cross-hairs of his own sniper rifle and pulled the trigger. "Come on, Fred. Just because Justine is a relentless viper doesn't mean all women are bad."

"Justine is the devil," said Fred.

"I don't totally disagree with you," said Greg. Justine looked like a cigarette dressed in a neon green tube top and daisy dukes—until she got pregnant. With not-Fred's baby. And pretended it was his for six months.

"But," Greg continued, "if people thought every man was like you...actually, maybe that's why I've been single for basically my entire life."

"Dear God, I think that's my problem too," said Bastian.

"Screw you guys," grumbled Fred. His screen turned black as he took a shot to the head, and he tossed his controller onto the coffee table. "My shift starts soon anyway."

Greg's screen turned black after a grenade blast hit him. "All right, I'm down, too." As he moved to stand, Bastian gripped his shoulder, moving him back into his seat as the game ended.

"Wait a minute, Greggie. You promise you're okay?"

"With...what?"

"Your heart. Passing out. That's...not good."

Greg looked into Bastian's eyes and could see the compassion of the seventeen-year-old boy who had just broken Fred Griffin's pointy little nose almost ten years ago.

That day, Fred had materialized from the crowd in the hallway and shoved Greg like usual. As Greg fell, his face slapped hard against the cold, unmoving floor. "I don't like your face, Normand," Fred said as he stood over Greg. "I don't like your hair." Greg braced for a kick, knowing it would be over quickly if he just let it happen, didn't fight, didn't speak. "I don't like your faggy glasses."

And then…

Sebastian Ortiz, transfer student who'd been promoted to captain of the track team, burst in like the Hulk and literally threw Fred into the lockers.

Greg had never met Sebastian. Even in their small 400-student school, Sebastian Ortiz was like an untouchable celebrity, a god. He'd held out his hand to Greg and smiled. "You're going to walk with me from now on."

Now, nearly a decade later, Greg still wasn't sure what to say. "I'll be fine, Bastian."

"You always say you're fine."

"Because I always am."

"Jesus, Bastian, if Greg says he's fine, he's fucking fine. Let him go to work. Meet this girl. Have her break his heart."

"Right," Greg said, standing and stretching. *Bad heart, so it's doubly funny.* "Thanks for the game." *This is going to suck worse than the* Batman & Robin *movie.*

CHAPTER 5

Greg breathed in the pungent smell of newsprint hanging over the narrow mazes of industrial metal bookshelves in Comics Inked. Compared to the near-mosh-pit that had crammed inside last night for an autograph, the store seemed empty tonight: just a young couple looking through old *Dark Heresy* supplements and the same five pre-teen skaters who showed up every Wednesday but never bought anything. Greg chuckled from behind the checkout counter at the front of the store as Val marched toward the boys in the back, each paging through the latest issue of *The Indomitable X*.

"This is not a library," Val grumbled, crossing his arms. With his shaved head, gauges, muscles, and tattoos covering both arms, he looked more the part of a bouncer than owner of a comic book store. An immigrant from Romania, Val had opened the store two years ago, and he'd changed so little from the previous shops he'd owned that Greg had felt transported back to the comic stores of his childhood when he'd first stepped in. No silly office toys or mugs, no area to sit and read or play board games, none of the things Greg had added to the store he'd managed in Texas.

"Aw, c'mon, Val, sir," one of the boys said, thick mop of hair hiding most of his face. "You'd never kick us out."

Greg shook his head and looked back down at the sleeved, autographed 100th issue of *The Indomitable X* in his hands. The last one. Stupid TIX looked just the same as he always did: big shiny faceless blob. *Congratulations, Mr. Eager,* thought Greg. *Your miserably boring superhero is flying across published pages while* Jude vs the Universe *is still just scribbles in my sketchbook.*

When *The Indomitable X* had first gained popularity a few years ago, Greg had been happy just to see kids openly reading comic books, not hiding them in *Guns & Ammo* like he had in school. But society's veneration for TIX almost made it more difficult for Greg to love comics. Comic book stores used to be safe zones, places where being the scrawny kid with glasses and a stack of comics was actually cool. But now there were TIX mobile games, TIX's Twitter page, TIX promoting life insurance on TV. And the TIXers guzzled all the marketing bullshit like overpriced organic juice boxes.

But she *likes TIX.* Greg looked up at the front door, obstructed by cutouts and posters. *Maybe. If she comes. She probably won't.*

"I built these bookshelves before you were born," Val grumbled at the boys, an exchange Greg knew would end—as always—with the boys buying one copy among them and journeying off to the skate park.

As Greg looked, one of the posters started to ripple, as if he were watching it dance under water. He rubbed his eyes, but when he opened them, the right angles of the bookshelves were loose and hazy. The floor lurched underneath him, and he stepped forward to steady himself on the counter.

Greg closed his eyes and focused on the beat of his heart, wild like Mad Mike and the Giraffefolk playing metalcore bass. *Not now,* he told himself. *I can't be sick. This has to pass like it always does. Usually does. All except that last time.* The room lurched again.

--

Zarah stared at the windows of Comics Inked from her car once again, knowing she was only steps away from Greg and the signed issue he'd promised just hours before.

She sighed and rested her head on the steering wheel. *What am I even doing here? I couldn't do this for Rob Eager, and I can't do it now.*

What would she say to him? Could she just walk in and pay for the comic and leave? Or ramble about the Indomitable X? Hamsters? Her semi-secret passion for cake?

The past?

Her heart thudded in her chest. She dug her nails into her stomach, trying to forget, but the crack of the shotgun, the jostling of the closet door handle—

"No," she said, and pressed her nails in deeper.

This was exactly why she didn't talk to Dad. Or her roommates in DC. Or even Behnam.

Fuck, she hadn't thought about Behnam Shirazi in a year.

Warmth rushed into her heart like a hot spring, then tugged and tore at it.

They'd dated for five years, but the distance of grad school—with Behnam in California and her still in Colorado—had grown a rift between them. And with her impending internship in DC, well, they'd decided to break up before it started. So Behnam never found out what had happened at the museum, or if he did, he'd never called. It was better that way, she thought now. Otherwise he'd have worried, watched her change, felt duty-bound to stand by her as the kryptonite of her memories still paralyzed her.

Zarah straightened her posture and looked at her reflection in the rear-view mirror. She'd never be Behnam's Zarah again, the girl playing guitar in the dorm hallway at Colorado University Boulder, slouched against the wall, writing songs about caterpillars building a racetrack to the moon. No, she was now broken Zarah, a guitar without its strings, hiding in her car from pedestrians.

And from Gregory Gilgamesh Normand.

"That's stupid," she said aloud.

Still looking in the rear-view mirror, she imagined her hair smoothing itself into ringlets, her freckles fading, the pale dim moon-glow of her skin brightening into a sparkle. "Enough of this. Z ran his EKG in the office," she said. "Z wants this comic. Z talked to him then. She can talk to him now."

She threw open her car door and stepped onto the sidewalk.

Smells of flowery perfume and aftershave and dog shit and car exhaust and shoe rubber and socks and baby powder and sweat and ice cream cones and lollipops created a whirlwind with the smattering of colors and overlapping tracks of voices and Zarah took a deep breath and

Z ran her hands through her hair
and Zarah pulled on her curls and
she spun the static around her fingers
and she inhaled and
she released a lightning bolt that stopped time
and she exhaled and…and everything stopped spinning. The ocean of people seemed suddenly distant, their eyes fixed on everything but her. She took another step.

She made it to the door—farther than she'd made it last night. No longer out front to announce his biography signing, the Indomitable X cutout was inside the display window, peering out next to Batman, Captain Marvel, and other superhero friends.

Just pull the door open.

But what if she just ran back to her car, drove back to her apartment, back to X the hamster, where she could hide until tomorrow and then—

He'd come back to the office.

She wouldn't have her comic.

She couldn't hide forever.

You can do this, Z, she heard her fans cheer, and she pulled the door open.

--

"Yo, Greg, you okay?" called Val.

Heart slowing to a steady, smooth jazz pace, Greg took a deep breath and opened his eyes to see a crisp, stationary room surrounding him. Val still stood cross-armed on the other side of the store. Beneath his thick eyebrows, a slight quiver in his bottom lip betrayed his concern.

Why couldn't my heart have gone wild at the damned doctor's? "Yeah, I'm fine," said Greg. "You know these little TIXers, they just make me sick."

Val's mouth curled into a smile just as the front door jingled.

Greg whirled around. Zarah stood wide-eyed in the doorway, her gaze darting this way and that. She was wearing the same yellow flowered blouse as in the office, clinging to her slim frame. But her hair, which had been pulled back into a tight bun earlier, now fell wild around her face like a lion's mane. Her brown eyes met Greg's, and she grinned like he was an old friend.

"You're—you're here!" blurted Greg. "I, uh, didn't think you'd really come." He scratched the back of his neck. *Idiot. You sound like a teenager.*

She nodded and took a careful step forward, as if she were entering a stranger's home.

"So, uh, did you want to look around? Or did you want any suggestions?"

"*The Indomitable X,*" Zarah mumbled.

"Right, right!" said Greg, stepping from behind the counter, autographed issue in-hand. She didn't walk toward him, only stared as if she were afraid the floor would burst into flame if she moved.

"It's the last one. My treat," he said, approaching her

and holding out the issue. He hadn't noticed in the antiseptic doctor's office, but here in the store, she smelled like pears.

As she took the comic with a slight smile, he held his hand up in a stage whisper as if to tell her a secret. "Even if you are a TIXer," he joked.

She raised a fiery eyebrow.

"Come on." He shook his head and laughed. "You have to admit—he's basically the most ridiculous superhero of all time."

"I worship him." Her expression was deadpan, like a nun asserting her belief in the Lord Jesus Christ.

Yikes. Good job, Don Juan. "He's just, you know..." his words wandered as he tried to save himself, "kind of unrelatable."

Zarah blinked. "Unrelatable?" Moving with sudden fluidity, she pointed an accusing finger at him. "You mean just because he doesn't swoon over some half-naked girl or have a sidekick who thinks he's witty, he's not relatable?"

Greg held up his hands in mock-surrender and backed away behind the counter. "A pointer finger's a dangerous weapon."

She glared.

Oh, she does not like jokes. You've dug your grave now, Greggie. "Okay, what I'm trying to say is, TIX has no weaknesses, no emotions, no relationships. He's devoid of a personal connection with anyone." Greg looked into the dead, black eye sockets of the TIX cutout by the door. "He's not human."

"Of course he's not human," she said as she stormed toward the counter. "He's an alien."

Greg wished he could start the whole exchange over again. "But readers can't relate to him."

"You're not supposed to be able to relate," she said, flailing her arms. "He's beyond relation. Graham crackers, he's a mass of light who defeats all evil. He doesn't have time for—"

"Uh, did you just say 'graham crackers'?"

Zarah straightened her posture and made tight fists. "No, why would I have said that?" Her cheeks flushed underneath her freckles.

"Um, you definitely just did." He leaned across the counter and grinned.

"Well…whatever. It's what I say."

Leaning back again, he said, "I mean, it's a sight better than 'Holy popcorn, Batman.'"

She laughed haltingly, loosening her hands again.

Not to mention it's adorable. "Listen, it's okay that you're a TIXer. But there's got to be more you like about him. Maybe you can enlighten me."

"Maybe you can help our customers check out," barked Val.

"Oh." Greg moved his focus past Zarah to the young couple standing behind her, *Dark Heresy* supplements and *The Indomitable X* issues in-hand. "Sorry, um, ma'am and sir."

They nodded and stepped forward next to Zarah, who shuffled to the side.

"So, *Dark Heresy*, huh?" he said as he rung them up. "Gotta love a good old sci-fi role-playing game. And TIX, he's my bud. You know." He handed them their bag and receipt. "Thanks for shopping at Comics Inked. TIX forever!" He started to pump his fist in the air, but feeling like the only nerd raising his hand in class, he coughed and lowered it.

Zarah giggled softly, pulling on a gold necklace tucked under her shirt. "I should probably go."

"Not until you tell me about TIX."

Her eyes shot toward Val and the skaters, all spectating grim-faced from across the store.

"Oh, they're not even real customers. And if Val won't kick them out, he's not gonna kick you out."

"C'mon," said the boy with the mop of hair. "Put Mr. Greg in his place."

"They won't judge you half as harsh as I will," offered Greg. "TIXers, every one of them, even Val."

This brought a hint of a smile from Zarah. She sighed and closed her eyes. "The Indomitable X," she began, then paused to breathe. "The Indomitable X is so much more than you give him credit for. Human lives are built on weakness and emotion and relationships, but he keeps saving this species he doesn't understand." She opened her eyes and looked at Greg. "He loves us that much."

Greg looked back at her as if for the first time. *She breathes life into that soulless sun amoeba.* "You talk about him like you know him."

She smiled. "I do. I've read every issue at least ten times."

Holy popcorn, Batman.

"But anyway," said Zarah, looking at the floor, "I really should go home. I need to feed my hamster."

Val coughed. *Ask her out*, he mouthed to Greg.

"Um," Greg ventured, "you like to eat and stuff, right?"

Zarah blinked.

"Ugh, okay, that came out totally wrong," Greg said to the counter, avoiding her gaze. He sighed and looked back into her dark eyes. "Look, you're so passionate about TIX that I obviously have tons to learn. And I, uh, kind of like to cook and can probably make the best grilled cheese you've ever tasted. Why don't you come over after my shift?"

Her eyes suddenly widened and jaw tightened, as if she were facing the Joker.

Great, now I've scared the shit out of her with a fucking grilled cheese. This is going swimmingly.

Val took a step forward. "Any guy can make grilled cheese," he offered, "but last month Greg brought in the best damned high-altitude cake I ever ate."

She pursed her lips as she considered.

"I get it. I'm freaking you out, right?"

Zara laughed and shook her head.

"And you laugh because?"

"Because I love cake. And I don't really like people, but I like talking to you. You make me feel brave."

He blinked at her. The truth behind her words—her love for TIX, the bit about feeding her hamster, love for cake, not liking people, *you make me feel brave*—in all these things, this obviously shy woman had laid her hand bare.

"Why?"

She shook her head. "I don't know."

"Greg!" shouted Val. "Get the hell outta here. I'll close up." He motioned to Zarah.

Greg grinned at his boss. "Oh, got it! Look, you seriously don't have to come over for dinner. You don't *have* to do anything. I'll walk you out."

He led her toward the door and stepped out onto Main Street, and the warm, dusty summer air hit his face.

"I want to come over for dinner," she said. "I just...I have trouble with people."

"Yeah, me too. Like I said when I met you, you're in good company with a weirdo like me."

She laughed. "You have no idea."

He looked at the sky and felt for a moment like he was stepping into someone else's life. New town. New job. New friend. And maybe...

In a moment of uncharacteristic boldness, Greg reached for Zarah's hand.

Air.

He looked to his side, but she'd vanished.

"I'm sorry," she called from the driver's seat of an old Volvo a few yards away.

"How did you—"

"I'm sorry," she said again, tears in her eyes. "I can't. I'm...." Her voice cracked. "I just can't."

He opened his mouth but didn't know what to say. As she pulled her car out of the spot and drove away, all he could do was blink.

I'll never see her again.

Ohmygod but what if I do at the doctor's office after I have a heart attack right here on the pavement?

I'm always, always, always messing this shit up. Good old Greggie. Expert with the ladies. Too reserved sometimes, too bold other times, never just right.

Oh, why hello there, pathetic pity party. Pull yourself together. She's just another TIXer.

But I'm pretty sure she might be awesome.

CHAPTER 6

The Great Gilgamesh grinned as he set a perfectly-triangular piece of chocolate cake with white confetti icing in front of Z. Smiling, she scooted her chair in closer to the tiny, distressed wooden table between them. Comics Inked glittered around them like the Colorado night sky with webs of Christmas lights canopied over the tops of its skyscraper bookshelves.

Z sighed and thanked the god Marathon for this second chance. Friendship was as alien to her as the planet Earth.

When she was a child on Marathon's Body—what the humans called "Planet Z"—a single crimson strand of hair fell before her face, gleaming in Marathon's light. She heard a voice in her head whisper, yenaioth, demon, and she tucked the blood-red strand of hair quickly back into her haiothe.

She was not like the Others, who had hair to match the wispy green plants of Marathon's Body. Z's hair matched His bright, shining crown of blood-red that brought them the Holy Light from the sky. When she was born, her father tried and tried to wash her mother's blood from her hair, rubbing his hands raw. But it stayed, mocking Marathon, as if her hair thought it was the hair of the god.

The Other children spotted her hair. "Yenaioth," they whispered as they surrounded her in the work yard. Ten, fifteen of them. "Demon." And then they tackled her and wrapped her in the thorny vine-hairs of Marathon's body, piercing her tender skin.

"It's bleeding! It's bleeding! Tighter!"

Her skin popped and become wet with blood, and she cried out, but they ignored her like always as they dug her grave, and then tossed her in like refuse.

"Let the darkness touch it," they whispered as they buried her.

Her father had stopped them the other times. But not this time. This was the time of the fire, when she became the Last.

Z's memories were interrupted as Gilgamesh nudged the cake closer to her and smiled sheepishly.

It was time for the truth. No more delays. With a deep breath, Z spoke the words she'd practiced with the Indomitable X all night. "I am sorry I left so suddenly yesterday." She paused and tucked a fiery curl behind her ear, never breaking eye contact. Eye contact was key, X had told her, to making human friends. But Gilgamesh's amber-green eyes, so different from the turquoise eyes of the Others, were already holding her attention. "I wish I could say that duty called," she continued, "that I was needed elsewhere, but that would be a lie. The truth is," she said as she poised herself for a bite of cake, "I know much of death but little of friendship. Where do we begin?"

Zarah stared at the sloppy slab of dry yellow grocery store cake in front of her. Across the break room table sat the Rhinocerkris, complete with conical birthday hat, a perfect horn on her surly head.

"You're exceptionally mute today," said Franklin beside Zarah.

Zarah continued to stare at the poor excuse for cake. Normally, she didn't mind that office birthdays had the worst cakes because it was, after all, cake. But after the promise of homemade grilled cheese and high altitude cake last night, it just seemed such a cruel reminder of her failure to be a balanced human being.

"It's just that I don't think I've ever seen you with a piece of cake actually in front of you," he continued. "Normally, in the time it takes me to focus my eyes, it's already en route to your stomach."

She cracked a smile and turned to look at Franklin, who was sporting his Muppets scrubs.

"Oh, come on. That half-assed smile makes me sad."

She shrugged. "I went to the comic book store."

His eyes widened, and he put down his fork. "You're kidding. You—Zarah Smith—went out among the gentry?"

"I did."

"And you saw Mr. Normand?"

"Yes. And talked to him. Debated about my favorite comic. He gave me a signed 100th issue—I didn't pay for it."

"What happened then? It can't be so bad as to refuse cake."

No, it was bad enough to inspire a cake hunger strike of epic proportions. "He invited me to dinner, but then I cried and drove away."

Franklin raised an eyebrow. "Are you going to call him?"

"How's the cake?" she asked, changing the subject.

He shoveled in another forkful. "Ucking dericious," he mumbled.

That evening, Zarah set a pan full of chocolate cake batter in her tiny oven and closed the door, while X squeaked from his cage on her desk across the room.

"Well," she said, squeezing out of her cramped kitchenette and side-stepping by her bed toward her desk, "someone ought to be eating good cake. It's not my fault the Rhinocerkris orders the driest, saddest ones." She reached her desk, slipped into her small red chair, and pulled her knees to her chest. At the slight hiss of the chair, X burst from his litter and scrambled toward the front of his cage. The summer evening sun still poured into the room.

Zarah reached for the chocolate box filled with sunflower seeds in front of X's cage and proffered one between the bars.

"Of course I didn't eat that cake," she said, resting her chin on her knees. "Franklin did, though. And the Rhinocerkris just licked off the icing as usual." She sighed, remembering her conversation with Franklin. "I know, I know. It's not about the cake. I need to apologize to Greg. But how do I apologize to a practical stranger for running away when my aversion to other humans is what made me run away in the first place?"

She stood and peered over X's cage and out her fifth-story window toward Comics Inked, three blocks away. Was Greg even there tonight? What if Thursdays were his night off? What if she made the whole trip for nothing? Or worse, what if there was another signing or big event, and people were crawling all over that place like ants, and then Greg saw her, and then she ran away again?

A quick G chord burst from the sidewalk below. The Chordinator, as she called the forty-something man in the acid-washed denim fringe jacket below, played Thursdays through Sundays. After a few moments of tuning, he started strumming the familiar G-C-G of "Brown-Eyed Girl."

Methodically, Zarah opened her desk drawer, extracted her ear plugs, and wedged them into her ears, but she could still faintly hear the lyrics and notes, transporting her back to college.

She remembered sitting underneath a tree outside her dorm at Boulder, tuning her guitar underneath the falling leaves, when a guy with a gray hooded sweatshirt, thick mane of black hair, and toothpaste-commercial-worthy smile plopped down next to her on the grass.

"Do you even know how to play that thing?" he asked, leaning back on his arms and stretching his legs out in front of him.

"Of course I do," she said, continuing to tune.

"Then play me a G-C-G."

She rolled her eyes.

"No, seriously," he said, leaning in close. He smelled like cinnamon and soap. "I want to sing you a song."

She scoffed. "That might work on the freshmen, but not on me."

"Do you know who I am?" He jumped to his feet. He stood like a superhero, hands on his hips, chest jutted out. Even through his hooded sweatshirt, she could see the outlines of his muscles. "I'm Behnam Shirazi. I'm a sophomore playing Marius in Les Mis here next month. They say my voice can make Medusa cry." He grinned wolfishly.

She shook her head and strummed an A minor. "Bad enough to make Medusa cry?" she asked with a smirk.

He dropped down to one knee and stared into her eyes. They were bright green, a perfect complement to the gold-brown skin of his face. "You'll see," he whispered, starting to sing the first line of "Brown-Eyed Girl". His voice was packed with all the power of a tsunami and clarity of a bubbling spring. His pitch, his volume, his enunciation—it all rose and fell with the waves of his words, at once bowling her over and setting her afloat.

"Well?" he asked, and as she weighed sarcasm against praise, a twitch in the corner of his mouth betrayed a shred of uncertainty. It was this twitch that started it. She felt her heart reach for him, for this handsome and talented and still uncertain stranger. *Don't fall for him*, she pleaded with herself.

"Acceptable," she said after a beat, "but I think some accompaniment will keep your pitch from wandering."

His eyes shot wide. "You're mistaken—my pitch is flawless."

She shrugged and, cracking a smile, began to strum G-C-G.

As she heard the Chordinator play on the sidewalk below, she wondered what Behnam was doing now. She and Behnam had played and sang together for hours that day—pop songs they'd loved in high school, country songs Zarah's dad had listened to while doing the dishes, musicals Behnam's mom had belted in the car on errands. As the sun had begun to set and stain the sky purple, they'd wandered over to the dining hall, then the planetarium, then back to their tree to play and sing some more. All the while, Zarah's inner plea of *don't fall for him* hushed quieter and quieter until after their third round of "Brown-Eyed Girl," when he leaned in for a kiss, and she snuffed the voice out.

They'd broken up five years later, a month before her internship. With him studying law in California and her continuing on at Boulder, the distance had already grown malignant between them, always taking more than they could give, expanding, first just between their homes but then between their aspirations, their thoughts, their conversations, until their spark just fizzled away.

But I can know what happened to him if I wanted to, she thought with a glance at her laptop—which she only used to order groceries, pay bills, and read *Indomitable* X fan fiction—buried under a stack of *Indomitable* X comics. After that day at the museum, she'd deleted all of her social media accounts, but she could still search his name. *There can't be that many Behnam Shirazis*. Her heart fluttered at the thought of seeing his face again.

Fingers tingling, she set her stack of comics on top of X's cage, to which he protested with a squeak. Why she hadn't thought to look for Behnam before, just to see a picture, a resume, anything that showed he was finally a successful environmental lawyer?

She paused as she opened her laptop. Maybe it was because he might not be a successful environmental lawyer. What if he'd sold out to corporate America, the thing they'd sworn to each other they'd never do? Sure, they'd sworn that when they were high and writing songs about saving the rainforest, but still.

Her computer screen flashed its background of Indomitable X flying over the DC landscape, and she opened her browser. "I just have to type his name," she said to X the hamster. "I know you never met him, but you would have liked him, and you would want to know how he's doing, too."

She poised her fingers to type and took a deep breath.

As she typed "B," she imagined him standing on the couch of his eco-friendly California home. She typed "E" and imagined his guitar in-hand. "H," and he was singing original kids' folk songs, "N," and she added a wife and twin girls dancing along with him.

What good would it do if she found his picture, his resume?

The British playwright Aphra Behn filled the screen.

"A," and she imagined him singing his vows at his wedding, the way he'd always wanted. "M," and she imagined him spending his honeymoon on a relief mission to Haiti.

Various Behnams who were not her ex-boyfriend filled the screen.

If she found him, wouldn't it just make her miss him? Miss playing her guitar that was interred in its case under her bed, dead, like the music it had played before everything changed, before that day in the closet, before Iris—

No, she wouldn't think about that.

She wouldn't think about Behnam, either. She shut her laptop.

The past was of no use. She dug her nails into her stomach. That was a different Zarah, a different life, and there wasn't a damned thing she could do to ever get it back.

"Fuck you, Chordinator!" she shouted at the window, standing up.

Then she sunk back into her chair, her hands shaking. She needed a distraction, something that pulled her out of this world and into a better one, a new one. She needed *The Indomitable X*. As she pulled her stack of comics from X's cage and placed them in her lap, the signed 100th issue from Greg stared back at her.

She traced Rob Eager's autograph with her fingers. Behnam, for the five years they'd dated, for all of the songs they'd written together, for all the midnight chats they'd had, had never tried to read comics. And Greg, who clearly held no love for the Indomitable X, had carefully saved her the last signed copy of the 100th issue.

Maybe there's no use in digging up the past, but Greg is here in Lark Springs, Greg is now, and Greg deserves an apology.

She pulled out her earplugs, re-opened her laptop, and looked up the number for Comics Inked. Then she ran her fingers through her curls, took a deep breath, reached for the old 1990s corded phone from her dad's basement, and dialed the number.

After a few rings, a gruff voice answered. "Comics Inked, this is Val."

"Hi, I'm…" Zarah mumbled and then became mute. *Holy Marathon*, what was she doing? She'd gotten so lost in the dreamy past that she forgot she was here, she was now, and she was broken. She needed Z, but there wasn't time—

"Hello?"

Zarah took another deep breath. It was just a phone call. She could do this. Zarah could do this. "I'm trying to reach Greg Normand."

"Oh, Greg? He went home sick."

Her cheeks flushed as the present colored itself in around her. Greg was a heart patient. Was it palpitations? Syncope? "Is he all right?"

"This is that girl from last night, isn't it?"

"Y-y-yes, that's me. How…how did you know?"

"How could I forget? Look, I'll give you his number. Talk to him. It'd make him feel a lot better."

"I…I…" she stammered as she twirled the phone cord

around her finger.

"Look, I'll give you his number, and you can decide whether you want to call him."

She scrambled to write it down, muttered a goodbye, and hung up the phone.

X squeaked, and Zarah fed him another sunflower seed. "I know, I know, I'll call him, just give me a moment so I don't throw up." Her pulse thrummed in her ears. She'd called a stranger. Now she was going to call Greg. Honestly, he was essentially a stranger too, but—

Get it together. She thought of the words she'd practiced last night with X the hamster. "I'm sorry I left so suddenly," she tested. Curling into fetal position, she dialed his number, pecking one button at a time.

The phone rang twice before his weak but familiar voice answered. "Um, hello?"

"Hi… this is…" She held her breath.

"Zarah?"

She exhaled. "Yeah."

His voice filled with energy just at that one word. "Really? Wow. Um, how are you? How'd you get my number?"

"I called the store," she said, trying to sound calm as her stomach went on a roller coaster. "Are you all right?"

She heard laughter and male voices in the background. She couldn't make out what they were saying, except she thought she heard her own name.

"Shut up, Fred! Damn it. Sorry, Zarah, um, my roommates are assholes."

Roommates? *Graham crackers*, she hadn't thought about roommates. If she'd gone over for grilled cheese and cake last night, they'd have asked questions about her job and school and why she'd never finished her MA—

"One sec, Zarah." Greg sighed. "Ugh, okay, I've locked myself in my room. Do you have roommates meddling in every iota of your life, too?"

"No roommates," she said. The last time she'd seen her

fellow DC Smithsonian intern roommates, they'd made a spaghetti dinner together and popped a bottle of five-dollar wine to watch *The Daily Show*. That next morning, they must have known what had happened—even though they'd all interned at different museums—because it had been all over the news. Before they'd come home, she'd thrown her things into trash bags, loaded them into her car, and left a month's rent on the coffee table. "Just a tiny apartment," she continued. "I'm kind of anti-social."

"You seem plenty social to me."

She bit her lip and thought for a moment. X squeaked and twitched his whiskers. "That's because talking to you is like talking to X."

She thought she heard a muttered "Fuck" on the other end. "You, uh, you, like, talk to—oh my god. You're like the most hard core TIXer ever."

Laughing, she said, "No, X is my hamster."

Silence for a moment. "So talking to me is like talking to a hamster."

"That's actually a compliment coming from someone who's anti-social."

"I'm a hamster."

"You're not a hamster, you're just friendly like one."

"I don't know if I like this," he said, but the warmth in his voice told her he was smiling.

Silence. What to say? She hadn't called him to say he was like a hamster. It was time to get it together, to be like Z and apologize.

"Cake," she blurted as the smell of chocolate began to permeate the room. *Marathon*, that wasn't what she'd meant to say. First the hamster bit, now shouting types of food—"I'm baking a cake," she finished.

"Really? Right now?"

"Mmm-hmm."

"Will it have sprinkles?"

She laughed. "That's such a specific question."

"No it's not—it's not any more specific than, 'Ooh,

what kind,' or 'Round or sheet cake?' Both of which, I think, are standard cake questions."

Maybe he really had baked the best high-altitude cake Val had ever had. "No sprinkles on this one," she said, feeding X a sunflower seed, "and it's a chocolate sheet cake with white confetti icing."

"Next question: Who's your sprinkle supplier?"

"Sprinkle supplier?"

"Oh, come on, Zarah. Aren't you a local? You must go to Gus."

"I'm antisocial, remember?"

"Right, right. Well then, Zarah," he said, an idea winding its way through the pitch of his voice, "I have a plan."

"And that plan is?" she asked, uncurling from fetal position and swiveling in her chair.

"A solution to the travesty that is your lack of sprinkle supplier. But first, is this your cell? 'Cause I was gonna save it."

The question burned a hole in her stomach. "It's my landline," she mumbled. "I don't have a cell."

"Oh yeah, the anti-social thing."

"Yes," she said, not wanting to admit her cell phone was interred, like her guitar, under her bed.

"Hey, no shame in that. Have a good night, Zarah!"

"Wait—what?"

But only a dial tone answered.

CHAPTER 7

Grab the paper. Grab the file. Open the prongs. Shove in the paper. Close the prongs.

Why can't I just be normal?

Grab the paper. *Are the words "I'm sorry" really so difficult?*

Grab the file. *"Hamster! Cake! I'm a veritable recluse! Blah blah blah!"*

Open the prongs. *Still, what's the worst that can happen? He never talks to me again? Isn't that what I want? To be alone?*

Shove in the paper. *At least the cake was good.*

As she closed the folder, Franklin walked into the file room, the frilly lines of his Cinderella scrubs weaving around his rectangular figure. He leaned against the counter and crossed his arms with a grunt. "Spill it."

"Spill what?" asked Zarah as she closed the prongs and moved the folder to her 'done' pile. "Also, you look ravishing."

"Why, thank you," he said, giving her a little twirl. "But don't get me off-topic. Did you call the comic kid?"

Zarah grabbed the next file with a groan. "Are you really that bored with your life?"

"Honestly?" he said, considering this question with scrunched eyebrows. "Yes, yes, I am. It gives me hope that you might not, you know, perpetuate in lonely monotony for eternity." He gestured to her entire body as if her very existence explained this statement.

Zarah frowned as she opened the file. It was Bob Stedford and *rigatoni legs*, for the love of Marathon. "I'm not lonely," she said. "There's X, my hamster. And my patients." She brandished the file like an award. "See? Not lonely at all. I have Bob Stedford."

"That's some sad shit right there," said Franklin, but as he spoke, a light sparked in his eyes. "Though it does almost answer a question I was going to ask you." He drummed his fingers against his clean-shaven face.

"What are you scheming, Franklin?"

"You'll see. Let's talk over takeout from Chinese Palace later. I'll drive."

The smell of sweet dough, soy sauce, and onions filled Franklin's Hummer parked outside of Chinese Palace, which was nestled into a strip mall between Marty's Discount Liquors and Lulu's Pet Grooming. Franklin rifled through the plastic takeout bag and handed Zarah chopsticks and box of shrimp lo mein.

"Has your scheme reached gestation?" Zarah asked as she opened her lo mein. The noodles, carrots, snow peas, and bok choy were browned to perfection, and her mouth watered.

Franklin opened his box of Hunan beef and started shoveling the food into his mouth before answering. "First, please tell me you called him."

"Graham crackers, Franklin, it's not that exciting." He stared back at her with raised bushy eyebrows, and she sighed. "Fine. It went like you would expect. I told him he was like my hamster, and then he said it was a 'travesty' that I don't have a sprinkle supplier, and then he hung up." Zarah took a bite of her lo mein, which settled onto her palate in a salty-sweet medley.

"Well, considering you're a reclusive hamster lady, I

hope he took it as a compliment."

"Now it's your turn," said Zarah, pointing an accusatory chopstick at him. "What's your evil plan?"

Franklin took a breath and closed his eyes. "Remember with me, Zarah, how you masterfully performed that EKG on an almost-stranger who is like a hamster?"

Zarah groaned. "It's not that funny."

"Wrong," he said, shaking his head, eyes still closed. "And it really was a masterful EKG."

A touch of pride snuck into Zarah's chest. It was true: she had placed all the electrodes in the proper place, despite the awkwardness of it being the Great Gilgamesh, aka adorable Greg.

Wait—do I think he's adorable?

"Now," said Franklin, his eyes still closed, "imagine that you start performing masterful EKGs once a day, then twice, and then more as you settle into the routine, until you just don't file papers anymore."

She frowned. What started as a vision of Zarah carefully placing electrodes spiraled into her standing in a room of empty shelves and holding a termination notice.

He opened his eyes. "I've convinced Kris and Dr. Desai to transition the office to digital files. I can give you my dissertation at another time, but I need you to understand—I'm going to make a place for you at the office."

Make a place for you?

Her breathing quickened. The lo mein shook in her hands as the world slowed on its axis.

My place is in the file room. It's safe in the file room. People don't talk to me in the file room. You can duck and you can hide and—

Shallow breaths.

What else can I do?

Where else can I go?

I can't even go into this goddamned restaurant.

Franklin set his food on the dashboard and placed his

hands on Zarah's shoulders. His touch was like a weighted blanket, and she slowed and deepened her breathing. "You can perform EKGs, Zarah," said Franklin. "You've proven that to me. We just need to prove it to Kris."

"But how could you—" she started to say, but cut herself off. She knew why he wanted to move to digital files. She couldn't expect the whole practice to stay behind, for patients to get less efficient care, just because she was…

Broken.

"I'm sorry, Zarah," he said, gripping her shoulders tighter. "But that leads me to my 'scheme', as you call it." He released her and gulped down another bite of his Hunan beef. "I have a meeting with Kris later this week. I'll talk to her. Our patients' files are like trading cards for you. You know their stats, their trivia. We need your expertise."

Her expertise was in curating ancient tablets and jewelry, in the history behind a shard of pottery.

But—maybe Franklin was right. Now she was a curator of files, a historian of a single slip of paper.

She pushed her thoughts away with a bite of shrimp. "Okay," she said, not sure what other option she had.

Later, back at the office, Zarah returned to find the Leaning Tower of Patient Files stacked precariously on her counter. She could hear Kris's froggy voice in her mind, "The pile is large. About to fall. Get it done." She filed reports for Mr. McGlucky, allergic to latex; Ms. Li, breast cancer survivor; Mr. Gonzalez, local jeweler; Ms. Reyes, Bronze Star recipient and mall Mrs. Claus. As Zarah filed report after report, she thought about what Franklin had said, about the files being like trading cards. That was the nice thing about Franklin—from day one, he'd seen through her invisibility cloak and simply decided to be her friend.

It was different with Greg. Something about him made

her want to peek out from under her invisibility cloak for a minute and say a quick "I'm here" before diving back under it again. Her heart swelled when she saw his wide and easy smile, heard the varying pitch of his voice, recognized his apparent desire to also have an invisibility cloak. And despite the fact that she barely knew him—and that he didn't even like the Indomitable X of all things— the little details of Gregory Gilgamesh Normand wrapped around her heart in a way that nothing had since Behnam.

But for what? Things with Behnam had died painfully after five years, and so far it had all been a disaster with Greg—her running away (twice), him hanging up on her. What was the point?

As the office slowed at 4:55 and she shelved the last of the files for the day, Zarah heard a knock on the file room doorway. She turned around to see the Great Gilgamesh— Gregory Normand himself—leaning against the doorframe as if he'd done so every day for the past decade.

Her heart went into the freefall of a rollercoaster dive. "What are you doing here?" she breathed.

"So," he said, rocking back and forth on his heels and staring at his Converse sneakers, "I may have been a bit too forward before by inviting you over to my place the other night."

"What?" Was she imagining him? Was this real? Was she going insane?

"You just met me, you know," he said, looking up with a shrug. "And given that you keep assuring me that you're anti-social, that was probably, like, a super weird invitation from me."

She opened her mouth to respond, but it was like one of those dreams when you can't speak—you've forgotten how. Instead, she stared at the lines of his red-and-black flannel shirt. *Would I make up this shirt in a dream? Am I actually passed out on the file room floor?*

"Still," he said, "I think you would love Gus's candy shop. And maybe—I mean, I'm really hoping—it's a little less weird for you to go to a public place with me than to come over to my apartment. And, like, I still want to make you dinner sometime if you decide that I'm not a total weirdo creep. If...that's something that you would like." He sighed and ran his hands through his hair. "What I mean is, come for a walk with me tomorrow. I want to see you."

His last five words cut through her dream. He wanted to see her: Zarah Smith.

"I want to see you too," she said, her eyes latching onto his.

His face lit up like a hearth. "Awesome sauce. Meet me at Comics Inked after work tomorrow. I'm working an earlier shift. Kaleido Kandy is a block away—we'll walk."

Walk? The word swam in her mind.

The vortex of pedestrians. The black hole of the evening dinner crowd.

I can't.

And that's exactly why I'm going to fail at Franklin's master plan to digitize files. I'm going to be left behind, the hamster lady who can't go outside, who can't talk to people, who can't...

Stop.

Stop being Zarah.

Be Z.

Z performed a "masterful" EKG. Z walked into Comics Inked the other night. Z can do anything.

Zarah imagined Z and the Great Gilgamesh, arm-in-arm, walking to the candy shop on a Sacred Sprinkle Mission.

She nodded, and Greg beamed.

"See you then," he said before he walked away.

CHAPTER 8

Outside of Comics Inked the next evening, the summer breeze carried the smells of sunblock and grilled hamburger as it gently wisped Zarah's curls in front of her face. The dusty brown peaks of the Rocky Mountains loomed in the west, and music from neighboring restaurants meandered down the street between the people and their dogs and their strollers.

Damn the May thaw. She pulled her gold chain out from under her shirt and rubbed the pendant, willing herself to become invisible.

She'd almost stopped at home for a pep talk with X the hamster, but after Franklin's insistence that doing so would only make it inevitable that she'd "stand up the comic kid again," she'd gathered Z into herself and driven directly to Comics Inked after work.

Greg emerged from the building with a grin on his face. "Hey there! Kaleido Kandy is two blocks that way and across the street," he said as he approached, pointing in the direction of the mountains. "Gus sells everything from chocolate-covered fruit to unicorn gummies to tie-dyed rock candy." As he listed each type of candy, he counted them out on his bony fingers. She felt warmth emanate from him as he reached her, and he smelled like deodorant and newsprint. As she breathed in his scent and his warmth, her body relaxed, the people around them faded away, and she released her medal. *This is his superpower*, she thought. *His amber Forcefield of Joy.*

He offered her his hand. "Don't worry," he said, wide grin spreading across his face. "I won't let the crowds suck you into the Centrifuge of Doom. Or something."

Oh my graham crackers in Marathon's tummy. His smile, his adorable awkwardness—it was almost too much. But even as her heart swelled, she hesitated. Remembering the day she'd met Behnam, she thought about how quickly they'd escalated from two strangers playing guitar on the lawn to a might-as-well-be-engaged couple spending every spare moment together. *It will be like that again*, she knew, especially now that all she really had was X the hamster. *You're already falling for him.*

"Too much?" he asked with a wince.

"No!" she shouted, grasping his open palm. A surge of energy flowed through her as if she had summoned Z. Electricity seemed to play on her fingertips as their hands intertwined.

He laughed and scratched the back of his neck with his free hand.

"I..." she said, not sure how to break the awkwardness. She looked around at the Centrifuge of Doom—as he called it—the people, the stores, the dogs. Oh! The sign for Comics Inked. Yes, that was a fitting topic. "When did you get into comics?"

"Ah, yes. I'll start at the beginning." As they stepped forward, two joggers brushed past Zarah on her left. *Graham crackers, I didn't even get to pretend I'm Z. Can I still pretend?* She gripped Greg's hand tighter.

"I was born a premature mixed boy in rural Texas." He paused for a moment and scrutinized her face. "You're supposed to laugh, Zarah. It's hardly the opening line to a legitimate epic."

Zarah gulped a breath and tried to smile.

"Anyway," he continued, "I spent my first months in the Neo-Natal ICU listening—not to children's stories—but to requests to Saint Jude, the saint of hopeless cases. You see, I'm the progeny of a deacon and a nun."

"Wait—are you being serious?"

He chuckled. "Mom was a novice nun—no vows, just a lifetime supply of Catholic guilt. She left the sisterhood before she met Dad in a bar. He was singing 'Levon' with his Elton John cover band. Now he's a doctor and a deacon at our church, and she's a teacher."

Zarah searched Greg's eyes for any hint of sarcasm behind his green thick-framed glasses. "Graham crackers, you're not joking."

He laughed and looked at the sidewalk as they stopped at a crossing light. "Oh, no. I wish I was. My sister and I were destined to either be very Catholic or very not."

"So which are you?"

The light changed, and they crossed Main Street. "Well, Joan's a tattoo artist that moonlights as a youth minister at my parents' church. I'm the miracle baby, the one Saint Jude helped save, but I haven't been to church in years." He shrugged. "I guess I believe in faith, not in religion. And I believe in *Jude vs the Universe*." He spread out his free palm in front of him to demonstrate the vastness of the concept.

In her nearly sixteen years of reading comics, she'd never heard of *Jude vs the Universe*. "What's that?"

"My comic. In my notebook." He smiled at her as if he'd saved her the last cupcake.

The world around her evaporated into ether except for Gregory Gilgamesh Normand and his halo of hair and amber Forcefield of Joy. "You're writing a comic?" she asked.

"I haven't told anyone besides my roommate Bastian." He tugged on her hand as they skirted around a double-wide stroller.

"What's it about?"

"Well, like, I think I might I owe Saint Jude a solid shout-out for not letting me die when I was a baby. So my comic's about him coming down from Heaven to fight— but wait! Back to your question." He shook his head. "I got into comics because saints are kind of like Catholic superheroes. But you get that, right?" He gestured to her necklace. "Catholic too?"

The question was so sudden that it seemed to paralyze her, and she stopped walking. As people swerved around them, her free hand crept up to her neck, and she felt the exposed pendant between her thumb and forefinger.

And then, like a monsoon, Iris's warm sing-song voice flooded her mind, the voice that had both cursed and prayed in Greek throughout the work day. Zarah could see the Mesopotamia curator's beautiful jet-black hair accented with strands of gray, like tinsel, fresh in her memory as if she were standing before her.

"It's a friend's," Zarah whispered as she tucked Iris's Saint Christopher medal back into her shirt. *This is exactly why I'm a hamster lady. People ask questions.*

"So," he said, and he tugged her hand to start walking again, "did you know he's the saint of bachelors? And travelers and toothaches and gardens and other stuff?"

They couldn't be talking about this. The buildings seemed to move in closer. "No." He was Iris's saint. Her lucky medal. She'd always taken it with her into the closet, to help her find things. *"I know, this is really Saint Anthony's job," Iris said as she stood in the closet doorway. "But Saint Christopher always helps me. Here, keep him with you into the closet this time. He'll help you find something for your thesis." As she pulled the chain from around her neck, her long, straight black hair shimmered.*

"Sometimes he's got, like, this dog's head in paintings. Not sure what that's about."

Iris placed the medal around Zarah's neck, and her hazel eyes glittered with excitement. "Good luck!" She smiled as she stepped out of the closet toward the exhibits and closed the door behind her.

"But anyway, we're here." Greg pointed to the sign hanging above the door to their left, which read in multicolored letters: "Kaleido Kandy"

Zarah looked around her and realized that they were surrounded by couples and strollers and dogs and skaters and joggers and sticky-handed toddlers. The smell of banana peppers, Alfredo, and soy sauce wafted from nearby restaurants. Lark Jewelers across the street glittered inside. Around her were dozens of conversations, dogs barking, babies crying. Iris and the museum fizzled back into a buried memory.

Greg stepped ahead of her and opened the door, which jingled its welcome. She could smell the fudge and watermelon and vanilla and salt pulling her inside and back into the present.

She stepped up to the threshold, just outside the door, and peered inside. Bins of candy hanging on the walls painted an overwhelming palette, like a child had taken a hundred colors of paint and splattered and smeared and hand-printed them all over the room, and where each splash of color had landed, candy had sprouted in its place. Zarah realized she was still holding Greg's hand and squeezed it tighter as she made eye contact with the bearded white man behind the counter. Apparently, Santa Claus ran Kaleido Kandy during the summer.

"You okay?" whispered Greg. "I promise I won't let go of your hand."

She swallowed. *Be like Z.*

"Well, come on inside, you two," bellowed the man. "Don't let the candy melt, now."

"How are you, Gus?" Greg asked as they stepped over the threshold and through the door.

"Just dandy. Pound of peach rings—the usual?"

Zarah smiled, coming back to herself. *The usual? Like Greg has been coming here every week for his "usual" pound of peach rings for the past seven years?*

Careful, Zarah, you're letting yourself feel too much.

Greg scratched his neck with his free hand. "Yeah, well, that'd be great, Gus, but we're gonna need some sprinkles, too."

"Perfect!" Santa Gus said as he slapped the counter. "I just got some new ones in!" Gus shuffled around the counter and past Zarah and Greg to some particularly vibrant bins of candy. "Our special for May is—" he paused for effect and waved his fingers in the air, "circus animals!" Gus scooped a bit of the circus animal sprinkles into his hand. He approached Zarah and Greg with his treasures. "Here," he said, pointing to one of the blue gems, "is the elephant. And here," he pointed to a pink gem, "is the tiger. And we have a lion. And of course, we can't forget the classic seal with his ball. But my favorite," he began to whisper, "is this one here." He pointed to a teeny orange flamingo. "I've never seen a flamingo in a circus, but boy, would I love to!" He sighed as he gazed at the animal sprinkles in his hand. "It's like my very own circus in the palm of my hand. Or on top of my cupcake. Or on my strawberry ice cream cone. Or even on my pistachio pudding!" Gus began to pick up the circus animals one-by-one and eat them.

Zarah squeezed Greg's hand. "I think X would like the circus animals."

"Are you sure?" Greg asked. "I mean, isn't it a bit unnatural for a hamster to eat an elephant? Or a flamingo?"

"A hamster?" Gus gasped, sheltering the remaining sprinkles in his cupped hands. "No cupcakes? No pistachio pudding?"

"I'm putting it on a cake I made the other night," Zarah interjected. She paused with surprise at the sound of her own voice in front of this stranger. She bit her lip, then continued, "A chocolate cake with white confetti icing."

"Ooh!" Gus began to bounce up and down. "Chocolate cake and confetti icing is a fitting home. Oh, it's where these sprinkles were made to shine!" He popped the last two into his mouth. "But what about this hamster?" he asked, furrowing his wiry white eyebrows.

"He's a very special hamster," said Zarah. "He's my friend, and he loves sprinkles."

"Well," Gus said, "I suppose a sprinkle fan is a sprinkle fan, human or not."

"We'll take a quarter pound," said Greg. He turned to Zarah. "Anything for you, Z?"

Z. The world stopped spinning on that single letter.

"What did you call me?" she whispered.

He cringed. "Um, Z?"

Her cheeks burned, but her lips parted into a smile. Z. To him, she was already Z. Hand-in-hand with him, she didn't need to pretend, didn't need to transform. Her smile crept into a grin. "I like it."

"Whew," Greg said with a laugh, "I couldn't tell, thought maybe I hit on a sore spot or something."

"No. I was just under the impression you had something against one-letter names." She winked.

"Oh, truly I do for a superhero like your beloved TIX. But, you're way more interesting than TIX. I'd say you're a tough cookie to crack."

Zarah thought for a moment. "Like a fortune cookie? What does that even mean?"

He shrugged. "I'll be honest, I got it from Morrow Maynard."

"Who?"

"A children's author, basically the only famous person in this town. *Can You Crack a Cookie* was Maynard's first big hit." He scratched his head with his free hand. "I might have Googled this place before moving here."

Gus forced an "ahem."

"Candy, right," said Zarah. "What flavor lollipops do you have?"

"Well," Gus said, shuffling around again, "we only have summer flavors." He reached a lollipop rack at the entrance to the store. "We have watermelon," he said, flicking the correspondingly-shaped lollipop like a magic wand, "piña colada, and peach."

"Peach," Zarah said.

"What a lovely flavor. A lovely flavor! Something you have in common with Greggie here," he said as he began to bag up the candy.

"You're my hero, Gus," Greg said with a smile. "How much do I owe you?"

Gus glanced at Greg and Zarah's intertwined hands. "Call it a gift from old Gus."

"Come on, be serious." Greg released Zarah's hand to open his wallet. And...the electricity of Z didn't leave her. Greg pulled a twenty-dollar bill from a duct tape wallet with a crude Batman symbol on the front. "I'll leave it in the tip jar," Greg said, "and you can't stop me."

Gus crossed his arms and looked to the right.

Greg snatched up the candy, put the twenty in the tip jar, and grabbed Zarah's hand. The bell jingled again as they stepped out of Kaleido Kandy.

"Gus is kinda silly, but I like him," said Greg. Around them swarmed joggers and dogs and children, but Zarah remained focused on Greg's smile. "I moved here just before Christmas," he said, "and I saw old Gus sitting in a sleigh in front of the Christmas shop in a Santa suit. He's, like, a Santa in the winter."

Zarah laughed. "I thought he looked like Santa Gus."

"I think he might, like, really be Santa. For real. You saw how he gets about his candy. Especially anything new."

As they stopped at a crossing light, a gray Schnauzer pawed at Greg's leg. He smiled and scratched his ears with his free hand.

"So I guess sprinkles are a big deal in the North Pole, then?" she said.

"Apparently, Santa's tastes are just as refined as your hamster's."

"I told X you guys would be friends!"

"You—what?" Greg raised an eyebrow and stopped petting the Schnauzer.

"I…"

"That's adorable, Z. I'd love to meet him. Honestly, I'd love to make you dinner."

Graham crackers.

"I mean," he said, staring at his shoes as they continued to wait at the crosswalk, "I get it if that's, like, way too forward."

"No," she said, and she realized this was it. This was the moment. This was when she would let herself start to fall with reckless abandon for the Great Gilgamesh and his comic in his notebook and his pound of peach rings and his knowledge of local children's authors. "I'm free tonight. Why not?"

"I, um," he sputtered. "Just need to pick up a couple things at the corner store a block past Comics Inked."

The light changed, and they continued up the sidewalk toward the corner store, talking about hamsters and comics, swinging their hands and laughing, briefly letting go to elbow each other or eat a peach ring. And for the first time in two years, Zarah didn't worry what the people around her were thinking, how frizzy her loose curls were, or even that she out in public. Instead, she felt like Z.

CHAPTER 9

Zarah hung up her keys at home at nearly eight o'clock, having driven ahead of Greg while he stopped for groceries. She looked around her apartment and suddenly felt nauseated. Every wall was plastered with *The Indomitable X* posters—except along her bed where she'd tacked stick-figure drawings of Z. Overflow piles of old *Avengers*, *Harbinger*, *Exiles*, and other comics too numerous to fit on her bookshelf stood in towers below her desk. On her bed sat Bunny the koala. At least her dad had successfully begged her to leave her *Indomitable X* bedsheets at home when she'd moved out.

She pulled on her curls and tried to imagine Greg—likely on his way now—in her apartment. "Oh my god, X, I'm an idiot," she said as she offered a sunflower seed to the hamster. "Maybe I can still call him and cancel?" But X squeaked in a way that said, *be brave*, or at least that was how she decided to take it, so she straightened her stacks of comics, hid Bunny the koala bear under her bed, and placed her signed 100th issue of *The Indomitable X* prominently face-out on her bookshelf.

A knock sounded at her door. She peered out the peep-hole to see Greg, grocery bag in-hand. "He's here," she whispered to X, then took a step back, breathed deeply, and opened the door.

Greg grinned once his eyes met Zarah's. "Victory!" he said with a fist-pump. "Um, your apartments aren't exactly in what I consider alphabetical order."

She laughed. "Sorry, I forgot. I don't have many visitors."

Greg scratched his head with his free hand while the other grasped his grocery bag.

"Oh, I'm sorry, come in."

He laughed as he stepped inside the doorway, between the kitchenette cabinets and bathroom curtain. As Zarah closed and latched the door behind him, he gazed around the room. "Wow, it's even worse than I thought."

Zarah could feel her face burning, but he only grinned. "I love it, Z! It's so nice to meet someone who loves comics as much as I do, even if you are a TIXer."

She frowned.

"Sorry, I mean it with love." His eyes widened as if he'd just peed himself in front of her. "I mean, not *love*, like, I'm not...oh God. Where can I cook this grilled cheese?" He squeaked his last sentence.

Zarah directed Greg to the kitchenette on his right, and he dumped out the contents of his grocery bag onto the stovetop. In front of him now lay two croissants and a package of brie.

Where was the 99-cent white bread? The perfectly-square American cheese? "What is this, exactly?" Zarah asked.

"This, exactly? This is the best damned grilled cheese sandwich you will ever, ever taste. Now," he cracked his knuckles, "you can't watch a master creating his masterpiece. It'll interrupt the magic."

"You seem amped," she said.

"Well," he said, opening the package of brie, "I told you before, I like talking to you. Even though talking to me is like talking to your hamster or something—oh, wait!

Where is this hamster who must be so awesome?" He put down the unwrapped brie.

"Oh—he's over here, at my desk," she said, gesturing toward the window on the far side of the room.

Greg side-stepped like a melodramatic detective between her furniture, then sat down in Zarah's red chair and leaned in toward the cage. In a way, it was strange having someone else in her apartment. But in another way—and what seemed to be the way of things with Greg—it was as if he'd been here a hundred times before.

X stared back at him, twitching his long-whiskered nose.

"Hey, buddy," Greg said, tapping the bars on the cage. "Apparently, we have a lot in common."

Zarah stepped behind Greg and pointed over his shoulder to the sunflower seeds in her chocolate box. "His treats are in there, if you want to feed him."

Greg swiveled around the chair to face Zarah. "You feed him chocolates?" he asked, raising an eyebrow.

"No," she said, not wanting to admit it had come filled with chocolates from her dad on the Valentine's Day after she and Behnam had broken things off. "I just use the box to keep them in. Here." She reached over him for the box, but lost her balance and grabbed his chest to catch herself. Pausing, suspended for a moment, she looked at her thin fingers spread across the *Teenage Mutant Ninja Turtles* logo on his shirt. Feeling the color of her face blend with her hair, she snatched up the box, regained her balance, and stood at attention.

"Sorry," she mumbled.

"Hey," he said, shrugging his shoulders, "glad I could, um, be here to catch you?" He sighed. "Yikes, that didn't come out like it sounded in my head. Uh, so sunflower seeds?"

"Sunflower seeds," she repeated, nodding. "Here." She opened the lid of the heart-shaped box and dropped a sunflower seed into Greg's hand. "You just feed him through the bars."

"All right," he said, swiveling back toward X's cage, and the hamster ripped the sunflower seed from Greg's fingers. "Wow, he's got some power."

"It's because he's named X," Zarah said.

"I'm sure the one-letter name has had an incredible effect on his strength."

X squeaked.

"Okay, okay," Greg said. "I think you'd better handle it from here, Zarah. I've got, like, a masterpiece to create for you, and all."

Zarah smiled as Greg got up and maneuvered back toward the kitchenette.

"He might actually be just a bit awesomer than me," Greg said as he opened the refrigerator.

Zarah sat down to feed X, wanting to ask the little blue-gray hamster what he thought about their visitor. It was like she was living someone else's life, like she was dropped in the middle of a date meant for some other girl, and things just kept progressing as if she wasn't broken.

She wanted to touch him again.

But that was creepy, right? To just go around touching people's chests?

Behind her, she heard sizzling and cracking from the stove top, and soon the welcoming smell of brie and butter emanated through the room.

"Where are your plates?" Greg called.

"Oh, let me get them." She stepped toward the kitchenette, where she realized Greg consumed all the floor space with his own two feet. Leaning and reaching into the kitchenette, she opened a cabinet and carefully lifted two porcelain plates from the shelf inside. In the past year, she'd started collecting "misfit" plates from online auctions: lonely only-survivor plates from broken sets. She currently held a holiday plate edged with tiny holly leaves intertwined with red ribbon, and a teal plate with a translucent gold glaze. One by one, she placed them into

Greg's outstretched hand.

And then they'd sit to eat...*where?* She had always eaten at her desk, sitting by X. But now, with a real person for company—

"All yours!" he said, handing her back the holiday plate, now holding a croissant sandwich of melted Brie.

"There's nowhere to eat," she mumbled, taking the plate.

Greg looked around the room. "Sure there is. Where do you eat?" He placed his sandwich on his plate and turned off the burner.

"At my desk, with X."

"Well, then, I suppose I can eat on the toilet," he said, smiling.

"No, that's ridiculous."

"I can stand."

"No, you sit, I'll stand."

"This is your apartment."

"But you're my guest."

Greg laughed. "What about your bed?" He poked her shoulder. "You aren't afraid of delicious crumbs congregating in your blankets, are you?"

Zarah felt her face flush and remained silent.

"Okay, crumbs are bad."

"No—it's fine," she said. *No, it's not fine! Sit on the bed together? When you're so cute and warm and I like your chest?* She stared at him for a moment, and then shakily stepped over to her bed and sat down on her lavender quilt.

He sat down beside her, making the bed bounce, almost causing her sandwich to tumble off her plate.

"Whoa, um, sorry," Greg said.

"It's okay."

Silence oppressively consumed the room.

"So, uh, I hope the sandwich is okay."

She hadn't tried it yet. She looked at his plate, and neither had he. *Marathon*, what was she doing? What had started out as wanting to apologize for ditching him had turned into him sitting next to her *on her bed* and her wanting to *touch him*. What was happening to her?

She pushed croissant flakes into a little pile on her plate. "I'm…" she mumbled, still staring at her plate, then whispered, "I'm sorry."

"Oh no, you're lactose intolerant, aren't you?"

"No," she said, laughing a little as the weight of the apology fell off her chest. "About the other night. I'm…" *What? More neurotic than Peter Parker?* "I don't know how to explain."

Greg grabbed her hand, and she felt the surge of energy run through her again, as if she really were Z and could conquer the world with the static in her hair. She looked up from her plate and into his amber eyes.

"I get it. Look, I'm a guy from a small town in Texas who loves comics and flannel equally. I mean, I'm literally dressed like a redneck Ninja Turtle right now. So," he said, raising his eyebrows, "a long time ago, I forced myself to be outgoing, make fun of myself, and meet friends. But when it comes down to it, I usually just feel awkward as hell."

"Really?" she whispered.

He nodded. "Especially around you."

It couldn't be. She couldn't make someone feel awkward, not when she was the queen of awkward.

He released her hand and paused. "Speaking of awkward, um, I really want to eat this sandwich, but my mom always told me to wait for your guest to eat first, and I know I'm, like, sort of the guest because this is your apartment, but also you're sort of the guest because I made this for you, like I'm the chef, or something."

Zarah laughed. "You're ridiculous."

He laughed too. "Eat your damned sandwich already!"

"Okay, okay," she said, taking a bite. As she bit down on the sandwich, the flakes of the croissant clung to the roof of her mouth and the warm, smooth brie oozed onto her tongue, mixing the flaky and cheesy goodness together.

Not stopping to speak, she quickly consumed the entire sandwich, which warmed her stomach.

She looked back at Greg, whose plate was still full and whose eyebrow was raised. "That was a pretty impressive display," he said. "Can't wait to see what you do to the cake."

"Oh, that's right," she said, jumping up from the bed and heading into the kitchenette. She dug through her refrigerator for the leftover cake. As she placed the container on the counter, Greg's voice asked close beside her, "So, um, was it okay?"

Zarah spun around to face Greg standing just outside the kitchenette, holding their dirty plates and grinning expectantly like he was awaiting Z's autograph.

"Yes. Amazing."

"Good." As he brushed past her toward the sink, the fresh laundry smell of his flannel made her feel like she was wrapped in warm blankets. Without enough floor space, their hips touched snugly. He put the plates into the sink beside her and began scrubbing.

"Greg, you don't have to do that."

"Oh." He paused for a moment and frowned. "Well, my mom believes that 'cleanliness is next to Godliness' so…I guess it's just habit." He continued scrubbing.

"You cook and clean? Your mom taught you well."

He nodded. "My parents are actually kind of awesome." As he rinsed the dishes, he asked, "Bathroom?"

"Behind the blue curtain." She pointed just across from the kitchenette. "I'll finish drying the dishes."

He narrowed his eyes for a moment but cracked a smile. "Fine."

As Greg brushed by her again toward the bathroom, she picked up the dishes and towel and began drying. Once she heard the curtain shut, she let out a deep breath. What was she doing? What was she hoping would happen? If sitting on the bed and holding hands made her near-mute, then how would—

Graham crackers, no. She hadn't even kissed anyone since Behnam. Since…

"So did you special-order the dinner serenade outside?" asked Greg as he emerged from the bathroom curtain. "Or is 'Sweet Caroline' a normal Thursday night treat?"

She listened and realized the guitar had begun. "The Chordinator. I tune him out most of the time."

"The Chordinator," he repeated, poking her in the shoulder. "Like he's a supervillain. You're hilarious, Z. Speaking of supers," he said, pointing to the wall by Zarah's bed, "Who's that?"

Zarah followed his finger to behold one of her stick-figure drawings of Z. Z's curls were merely squiggles in red pen, her eyes two black ink dots inside a scribbled mask, her dress yellow highlighter.

Classic. I remembered to shove Bunny under my bed but not hide my infantile drawings of my imaginary alter-ego. "Oh, no one," she answered.

He narrowed his eyes and stepped toward the bed. "Don't 'oh, no one' me after I've told you my whole life story plus *Jude vs the Universe.*"

Zarah's body wanted to retreat inside itself, to hide up in her brain or her curls, or anything. Greg wasn't supposed to know about Z.

But, there was something comforting in peeking out from under her invisibility cloak, in sharing just a piece of something with someone real, someone human, someone not X the hamster, someone who—unlike Franklin—would get it.

"It's Z."

"Like…like I've been calling you all day?"

She nodded.

"So it's you as a superhero?"

She nodded again.

He squinted his eyes and adjusted his glasses. "You're a heck of a lot cuter in real life, that's for sure." He shrugged and rocked back and forth on his heels. "So. What's she do?"

"She's…an alien," she offered.

"Like TIX. Okay."

Silence.

"So what's, like, the big thing she's famous for? Her moment of greatness, if you will?"

The whole world stopped. Z's moment of greatness was in the closet. The Babylonian storage closet. Where Z saved them. But—

No.

"It's complicated," she whispered.

"Oh, so it's like that," he said with a grin that drove back her memories and shoved them into her guitar case with the rest of her burdens. "How about I bring over my *Jude vs the Universe* concept art sometime? Then you can see what a mess it is, and talking about your ideas won't seem so bad."

So he wanted to see her again. *Is that good? Bad? Well, of course it's good. Things are going smoothly, right?*

Do I want things to go smoothly?

Things going smoothly means someone else in my apartment.

It means I can't hide.

But it also means I'm not alone.

"First, let's finish decorating this cake," Zarah said as she opened the plastic container.

"Oh, that's right, we have a surprise for you, little guy!" Greg walked over to X's cage and dug through his bag of sprinkles. "How do you feel about eating a little yellow elephant, buddy?"

X's tiny paws snatched the sprinkle from between Greg's fingers.

Greg turned back to Zarah in the kitchenette. "Is that really the spirit of TIX inside that little guy?"

X squeaked.

"My apologies. I meant *The. Indomitable. X,*" Greg said, pausing dramatically between each word and flashing his hands as if displaying the title on a billboard. Then he bowed, "Your greatness."

Zarah chuckled. "I'm glad you're beginning to realize his majesty."

"If anyone can teach me to see TIX for what he really is, it's you."

Her cheeks flushed as he walked back toward her.

"Nice technique on the icing," he said, leaning over her shoulder. The warmth of his breath, his closeness, and his fresh laundry smell made her feel like a teenager again. "It looks like a creamy cloud."

"That's the intention," she said. "So who's doing the honor? With the sprinkles from our sacred sprinkle mission?"

"First of all," he said, "you're the cutest. Second of all, I want to scatter the sprinkles."

"You scatter ashes, not sprinkles. You bestow sprinkles."

"Um, are we baptizing the cake?"

"Greg, it's a very sacred process, just like our mission." She snatched the sprinkles back and unzipped the plastic bag. "These orange flamingos and blue lions bring this cake into its true destiny."

Greg scratched his neck, lips parted as if to speak.

"This yellow elephant," she said, pulling out a single sprinkle, "sanctifies and—" Zarah's lip began to quiver "—blesses—" she began to giggle uncontrollably.

Greg pursed his lips and shook his head. "You're ridiculous, you know?" He pulled the elephant from her fingers and dropped it gently onto the confetti icing. "Now he's beee-stooowed." He flicked his fingers as if he had performed magic.

She continued to giggle, and loose red curls fell around her face. Greg put his arm around her waist as it shook with laughter. "Only you, Z."

Her waist stopped shaking as it fell against his. Suddenly, the pit of her stomach felt—what? Not nauseated, but like all the warmth of the red sunset beamed inside it, like the warmth of the grilled cheese, and she felt that if she breathed in, red sunlight would fill each hair on her head.

With one hand still on her waist, he brushed the other through her loose curls and rested it against her cheek. "I can't help it." And when his mouth reached hers and pushed it open, she felt all the sunlight in the universe pass between them.

"You taste like peach," he whispered, just before she pulled him back to her.

CHAPTER 10

Canopies of Christmas lights twinkled like a firefly family reunion over the seven-foot-tall maze of bookshelves inside Comics Inked, illuminating the store just enough to set the Great Gilgamesh's eyes aglow.

Z wondered at the warmth she felt in her chest when she was near him. It was greater than the warmth of the Indomitable X's cheek against hers each time they embraced, Father's arms each time he had saved her from the Others, even the radiance of Marathon's Crown that had brought the Light each day.

She touched her hand to her chest where the top of a red-orange Z was embroidered across her yellow dress, and she suddenly feared the threads would burst with light reaching for the human sitting across the wooden card table.

What did it mean?

What did it mean when he'd pressed his lips against hers last night? When he'd grinned and squeezed her hand? When he'd whispered "Good night" and tucked a fiery curl behind her ear?

She knew what it meant. But…

In the twinkling light, she could make out the frailness of his shoulders under loose blue flannel, the boniness of his fingers as they clutched a pen and notebook, the sallowness of his otherwise dark skin. She would break him, she knew. Not just with the lightning in her hair. She'd watched these humans' movies and read their books, and knew that if he latched onto the light trying to burst from the Z on her dress, he'd be drawn like a moth to the flame, only to be incinerated. Or he'd wilt and die like a flower in winter when she turned her light away.

She would turn away, eventually.

Z, for all her power, was still fragile, after all. The buried Demon of Marathon. The Last. The Pariah.

And what if she was the one latching onto him? What if she faded into nothing but a cheap sidekick, or worse, the damsel in distress? For two years she'd longed for someone to strengthen her spirit, be it the Great Gilgamesh, the Indomitable X, or Marathon Himself. To be tempered on this strange planet.

Loving him would end in either his immolation or her light being suffocated and snuffed out.

"I have to come clean, Z," said the Great Gilgamesh. His eyes darted around the room for a moment as if trying to count the lights overhead. Finally, they locked with hers. "I'm not the Great Gilgamesh. Gilgamesh is just my middle name." He looked down and fiddled with his pen. "I'm just Greg. Gregory Gilgamesh Normand."

Watching him bite his lip and stare, limp-shouldered, down at his pen, Z was reminded of Zarah Smith, the frizzy-haired, mousy file clerk persona she wore to become invisible.

The Z on her dress began to glow with empathy. "I'm not always Z, either. Sometimes I'm just Zarah."

"That's different," he said, looking up in awe. "I'm really Greg; I just pretend to be the Great Gilgamesh. You're really Z and only pretend to be Zarah."

The Christmas lights in Comics Inked grouped together into overhead track lighting. As the lighting shifted, Z could see her reflection clearly in Greg's glasses: perfect ruby ringlets, shimmering skin, confident dark eyes behind a red-orange mask. As long as she was Z, as long as she was a superhero, Greg would burn by her light or put it out. But if she were human, if she were Zarah Smith, they'd be vulnerable together. Broken together.

She reached up to her face and pulled off the mask. A pale, freckled girl stared back at her from the reflection in Greg's glasses.

It wasn't real, she admitted. Gilgamesh. Z. They were ideas in her head, just like they always had been.

"I'm not Z either," she responded. "Z and Gilgamesh don't exist." Her hair burst into a frizzy mane. "We're just Greg and Zarah."

And then suddenly, the pen and notebook in Greg's hands morphed into a plate of stuffed pasta shells, and he grinned that classic Greg grin and said, "Want some conchiglie?"

Zarah, ripped from her reverie, blinked at an office visit report under oppressive fluorescent lights. Blurred words in black ink gently sharpened into focus.

```
Patient complained of stomach
bloating like a pasta shell.
Insistent on using specific term
"conchiglie."
```

Slowly, Zarah became aware of the peeling mauve wallpaper and dingy metal shelves surrounding her. Beneath the report was an open manila folder, edges worn from use.

```
Last Name: Stedford

First Name: Robert
```

"Of course it's you, Bob," she said aloud. "Pasta shells? Stomach bloating? That's not even what we do here."

"Dear god, she's talking to the files," Franklin said, shaking his head as he entered the filing area from the hallway.

"Franklin, read this. Really." Zarah flung the file at him, and he caught it against his chest. "Mr. Stedford's gone beyond last week's 'spaghetti noodle' sensations and moved onto advanced Italian pasta shapes. We need to refer him for a psych eval."

Franklin shook his head as he scanned the paper. "Oh, Bob, what would we even do without you?"

"Take a nap? Get some coffee? Write a musical?"

Franklin looked up and cocked his head. "You're in a mood this morning."

"Because I'm joking about writing *My Heart is Pasta: The Bob Stedford Musical?*"

"Yes, you have far too much energy for a Friday." He raised an eyebrow. "What are you hiding?"

"Nothing." She returned to filing papers.

"Oh, shit," he said, "you hooked up with that comic book nerd!"

Zarah straightened her posture and fought a grin. "I did not 'hook up' with him."

"Well, you sure as hell did something. Jesus. I don't actually think I've ever seen you smile like that before." He shuddered. "It looks unnatural on you."

"We just ate cake," she said as she moved another file to the right.

"That is so sick and twisted, I don't even know what it means."

"Franklin!"

"So you met up with him, then?" Franklin leaned against the counter.

"Yes." Grab the paper. Grab the file.

"And..."

"And we went on a walk. Bought sprinkles." Open the file. Shove in the paper.

"So are you going out with him again?"

Shut the file. "I don't know, Franklin. I haven't dated anyone in a long time. What if it doesn't work?"

"What if it does?" he said.

Exactly.

"Well, I actually had purpose in interrupting your daily filing routine beyond prying into your personal life. Kris sent me to bring you to her office."

Zarah stopped filing and looked up at Franklin, who had closed Bob Stedford's file and slid it under his arm. Their conversation. The digital files. She'd forgotten.

"Come on," he said, motioning her out of the room.

Kris's office was lit solely by a desk lamp and muted bands of sunlight peeking through closed blinds. On the mauve walls hung framed oil paintings of a tabby cat as famous subjects: *Whistler's Mother*, *The Girl with the Pearl Earring*, *George Washington Crossing the Delaware*, all with a cartoony style of thick black paint outlining the cat's features. The room smelled of lilacs.

The last time Zarah had been in this room, she was signing re-hire paperwork.

Facing Zarah from behind a mahogany desk was the Rhinocerkris, wearing her usual gray suit and tapping her fingers together like the quintessential supervillian.

The Rhinocerkris's eyes locked on Zarah's, the villian's x-ray vision able to see into poor Zarah Smith's brain. Little did the Rhinocerkris know that by night, this timid file clerk was Z—her arch nemesis—and that now she was gritting her teeth as she held back the static buzzing in her hair.

"So, Zarah," said Franklin, "I was telling Kris about how you've been reading the files and helping me with EKGs."

Zarah's palms started to sweat. Franklin knew she wasn't supposed to be reading the files. Kris had expressly told her not to, and she was always pointing out how tall her piles of files were. *But even though Z was far more powerful than the evil Rhinocerkris, she could not let her identity slip over a simple human workplace power struggle.*

"Uncertified," said the Rhinocerkris in monotone.

"Yes, there is that," said Franklin. "But, look." He laid Bob Stedford's file in front of Kris. "Quick—Zarah, what is Mr. Stedford's date of birth?"

"January 1st, 1953," she answered, picturing his file in

her mind, not needing to call upon her superpowers due to the absurd frequency with which this man's file had crossed her vision.

"And what are his symptoms?"

She listed off the various pasta maladies. "But that's just in the past week or so."

"See, Zarah knows our patients," said Franklin. "There's no one better to help me with EKGs, even if they are certified. And if you're going to go forward with digitizing the files, Zarah's going to need a place here after everything is transferred over."

Tiny bolts of lightning zipped from Z's hair of its own accord.

I still can't even walk by myself.

Kris rubbed her chin. "I'll consider it."

Grab the paper. Grab the file.

Franklin's hair-brained plan is never going to work.

Open the prongs. Shove in the paper.

I'm just going to wind up unemployed and have to move back in with Dad.

Close the prongs. Grab the paper. Grab the file.

Focus on tonight. You'll see Greg again.

Open the prongs. Shove in the paper.

Greg used to be just another one of these files. Syncope and palpitations. Normal EKG. Franklin's right—I know these files.

Close the prongs.

But he's not just a file anymore. He's Greg.

Greg is sick.

The realization hit her like the crash of a wave.

But it can't be too serious, right? The EKG was normal, after all.

Her blood rushed behind her ears, and the file shelves seemed to loom over her.

No, he can't be sick.

Yesterday he'd walked to her apartment, to Kaleido Kandy, back to his apartment. He'd been fine. Totally fine. Laughing and joking.

He's not sick.
Grab the paper.

CHAPTER 11

The piano and synthesizer of Neon Modem's "Flowers in Fingerpaint" lulled through Greg's ear buds as he sat cross-legged on the bed in his mostly-unadorned bedroom, save for the signed Sticky Chewing Gum, Shays's Rebellion, and Red Clove Ghost posters framed on its cracking white walls. He rested his face in his palms and frowned at the spiral-bound sketchbook laying open on his lap. Drawn in colorful ink was a sinewy, bearded young man in a tattered sackcloth robe, accented with the repeated gold-threaded Hebrew word for "hope" around the hems. The man's sandaled feet hovered just above the ground. To each side of his body spread an elegantly-feathered gold wing, creating a wingspan three times his height. But what held Greg's attention was the stark white space between the angel's hair and beard. Three months of sketching, and Jude's face remained Greg's kryptonite.

"And I thought TIX was soulless," Greg muttered to himself. "At least he has a face." With a sigh, he flipped past his drawings of the Universe's body of planets and nebulae, the City of Jerusalem rebuilt in Heaven, and the scuzzy cityscape of Purgatory, USA, to his latest installment. Greg's frown twitched into a smile as he beheld a slim-figured redhead whose curls swept away from her lightly-freckled face, which was adorned with a tiny red-orange mask. She stood confidently with her hands on her hips, a hint of mischievousness buried in her Mona Lisa smile. Her outfit was merely a giant red-orange Z strapped across her breasts, diagonal down her toned stomach, and around her front in a micro-skirt.

She looked like a classic super-heroine, but something felt off. Disingenuous. This wasn't how Zarah had sketched her concept for Z. Greg shook his head. "She's gonna murder me if she sees this."

When Greg had come back from Zarah's last night, Bastian was already asleep and Fred was still at work. Now it was past noon, Bastian had left for work before dawn, and Fred still snored like an 85-year-old pipe smoker with sleep apnea from his bedroom. *Why can't they be around when I need them?* he thought, staring at the drawing in his lap. *I kissed her. I haven't been with a girl in years. What do I do next at 26?*

Not counting painfully awkward third base in the back of his dad's car with Eve Myers after senior prom, Greg had only been with two other women: once with Stoner Daisy, who he'd been fairly certain only slept with him because she owed Fred money, and seven months of weekend-fucking with Charm whom he'd met at Comicpalooza.

But Zarah wasn't Stoner Daisy or Charm.

What if Zarah wants to wait, take it slow? Continue my prolonged near-celibacy and live out my craven sexual fantasies by illustrating them? And what if she wants more? What if she shows up naked at the door and pulls me inside and starts ripping my clothes off—then what? Lie down and let her pummel-fuck me like Charm? Climb on top and hope she doesn't look as horrifyingly bored as Stoner Daisy? Ask, "Are you okay?" over and over like I'm trying to decipher Eve Myers's anatomy in the back of Dad's car?

Shit! Why don't I know this?

Now that Fred's not with Justine, he just serves free drinks to girls and pretends he starred in local indie cowboy movies back in Texas. And before he came out senior year, Bastian just told girls he was waiting for marriage and they threw themselves at him.

Why the fuck is Fred still sleeping?

It's never going to work. Nothing is ever going to work. Might as well become a priest now and make Mom and Dad extra proud.

Someone thudded at his door. "Yo, Greg!"

Fred? "Finally!"

"Hey, it's your day off, right? Get the fuck out here and help me get through this *Soldiers* mission."

"Fred, I can't. I mean, I need your help with something," Greg said, staring down at Z's carefully-sketched cleavage.

"With what?" Fred opened the door and stood with a game controller in his hand. The greasy blond hair hiding his eyes blended with the unkempt beard on his face. His white undershirt was covered in cheese curl dust smears that could serve as viable fingerprints in a forensics crime lab.

"You look terrible," said Greg, pulling out his ear buds. "I mean, more than usual."

Fred stepped into the room and sat on the edge of Greg's bed. "I had to talk to fucking Justine for an hour last night."

Fucking hell. Not Justine again. Greg remembered when they were back in Texas and he ran into Fred pushing a cart full of baby bottles and diapers at Target. "Justine's pregnant!" Fred had said with a nervous grin, eyes watering so that Greg had been unsure whether Fred would tear up with pride or crumble into a crying, terrified mess. A few months later, he'd called Greg from the bathroom floor in Porky's Bar, sobbing incomprehensibly. "Fucking whore," was all Greg could make out when he'd arrived with Bastian to pull Fred off the floor.

"Why the hell is she calling you now?" Greg asked, back in the present.

"Typical Justine." Fred's bloodshot gray eyes peeked through his bangs. "She was all, 'I miss you. Come home. I think I still love you.' Whatever, eat my ass, Justine."

"Wait, she wants you to move back to Texas? Why?"

Fred started laughing, or crying with a fake smile, Greg wasn't sure. "Get this," said Fred, "she wants me to take care of her and Justin's kid. Isn't that the fucking stupidest thing you've ever heard in your life? Bitch cheats on me with some dude who has practically the same name as her, gets knocked up, pretends it's mine for five months, and wants me to come home and take care of their little bastard now that they broke up. That's bullshit!"

Christ. "I'm sorry, Fred."

"Whatever. So you gonna help me finish this mission?"

"Yeah, um, sure, let me just put my sketchbook away."

"Wait, who the fuck is this, Greg?" he asked, eyeing the drawing of Z.

Greg slapped the sketchbook shut. "Um, just something I kind of started working on for Zarah."

Fred yanked the notebook out of Greg's hands and began flipping through the pages. He stopped on a page, and his face lit up like Christmas morning. "Whoa. Is this the chick you're sleeping with?"

"We're not...."

"It's only a matter of time, man. You know those closeted nerdy girls do the kinkiest shit."

Damnit. Motherfucker. Shit. "They do?"

Fred rolled his eyes. "So does she look like this?"

Greg looked at the drawing in of Z in Fred's hands, her breasts and hips nearly popping off the page. "Um...sort of," Greg mumbled.

"Damn! I mean, damn Greg!" He punched Greg in the shoulder with his game controller. "Does she dress like this?"

"No," Greg said, snatching back the notebook. "Of course not. No one dresses like that."

"Justine does," Fred mumbled.

"Well, no one but Justine dresses like that."

"So…does she know you draw fucking half-naked stalker pictures of her?"

"It's not a stalker picture."

"It sure as hell looks like one."

Greg paused to take in the whole of Z's slim but amply-endowed figure on the page. "You think this would freak her out?"

"Hell yeah! It even freaks me out a little."

Greg sighed and collapsed backward on his bed. "I don't know what to show her then."

"What are you talking about?"

"We're, uh," Greg began, staring at the water-stained ceiling, "we're working on, like, this comic book together. Maybe. I think. I don't know. I hope we do."

"Oh, hell no. She hasn't gone running yet?"

"Technically twice, but that was just from me. This is a drawing of a superhero she made up herself."

Fred leaned back and peered down over Greg's face. "It's not her, then?"

"It is, but her as a superhero."

"So her body doesn't really look like that."

"It might."

Fred sat up and shook his head. "You are way too much of a gentleman, Greg. Comic books and clothing."

"Yeah, well, I don't know. I'm supposed to show her my concept art."

"Concept art? How'd you manage to get her to go out with you talking like that?"

Greg shrugged.

"So…are you ready to run this fucking mission yet?" Fred leaned back again, his hopeful eyes masked by his greasy blond mop of hair.

Greg sighed. *Fuck it. This is just making me feel worse, anyway.* He pumped his legs in the air to roll forward and jump off the bed. "Yeah, let's do this."

The electric guitar music signaling "Mission Complete" circled on repeat through the living room as Greg and Fred lounged on the lime-green sofa, cups of noodles in hand.

"I'll tell you what, Greg," said Fred, pulling noodles from his cup with a fork, "you're the best damned sniper I've ever played with."

"Thanks, Fred," said Greg, just before taking a bite of his own noodles.

"I mean, Bastian's great at explosives on this game, but you can pick off any motherfucker you want." He slurped a mouthful of noodles. "I'm glad you moved here with us. I know I used to be kind of an asshole to you and all."

Greg smiled and shook his head. "I let that go a long time ago, Fred. Senior year, when Bastian came out and you beat Joe Casey into oblivion for being a shit about it."

"He was a total shit, dude." Fred laughed. "But so was I. To you."

Greg leaned forward and put his cup of noodles on the coffee table. "What's going on, Fred?"

Fred shrugged and stared at his cup. "I mean, I don't know man. You were the first one there for me when…the whole Justine thing. Sometimes I wonder why the hell you're nice to me, why the hell you even moved here with us."

Greg opened his mouth to speak, but Fred continued, "I know you and Bastian have always been friends. But when he got a sweet job here, Justine was a month away from popping out Justin Junior, and I needed to get the hell out of Wilford." He looked at Greg. "But you left a good life to live with your best friend and some asshole you tolerate."

Greg sighed. "My life there sucked way more than what I have now."

"From running a store to hourly clerk? That seems like bigger suck to me."

"I don't know…I guess I felt like…." He paused as he

remembered the moment he'd decided to move. Wolff-Parkinson-White Syndrome. Not much to worry about at the moment, just had to keep an eye on it. Lots of people had it, even Marilyn Manson, or at least that's what Google had said. Still, he'd felt the calendar moving closer and closer to his 26th birthday, when he'd be dumped from his parents' insurance.

But he was the premature son of a deacon and a nun, the boy Saint Jude had personally helped save. He couldn't throw all that work away just because Texas scorned public health care. So when Bastian had said he was moving to Colorado, and another Google search had showed Greg he could afford health insurance there, the choice had been obvious.

Fred and Bastian just knew he'd had some doctor's appointments, but not that he had a real disease with a name that seemed to be flaring up every couple days now instead of twice a year.

"Like I said, I forgave you eight years ago, Fred."

Fred straightened his posture. "That's cool, man. And, let's face it, you're doing better than Bastian and me combined: you're the one with the hot girl wearing a Z." He held up his noodle cup to Greg and they clinked. As they laughed, the banjo and tambourine of Red Clover Ghost's "Dark Haired Queen" sang from Greg's jeans pocket.

Fred raised a blonde eyebrow. "Whose ringtone is that?"

"Uh…" said Greg, grin involuntarily burning on his face as he held the phone. Smiling back at him was a picture he'd taken of Zarah last night, hand covering most of her face.

"Oh—it's her! It's the Z chick!"

"Shhh…please don't ruin this for me."

Fred put up his hands and began backing away in mock surrender. "Whatever, dude. I'll just be in my room carving at Justine's picture with a steak knife some more."

Greg shook his head and pressed "Accept."

"Hey, Zarah," he said, fishing for freeze-dried, water-logged vegetables with his fork.

"Are you still coming over tonight?" she asked, excitement pouring through her voice.

Greg's grin faded as Fred's words echoed in his mind: Closeted nerdy girls do the kinkiest shit. What was he supposed to do? Kiss her at the door? Grab her ass? Try to pull off her shirt? What if last night was just a fluke and she was going to break up with him before they even started dating?

He forced himself to smile again, hoping the action would make his voice sound optimistic. "Yeah, definitely."

"Perfect, I can't wait to see you."

Ohmygod, what if she's naked at the door waiting for me to become the closeted-nerdy-girl-pleasing expert. Distract her. Distract her now, damnit, before she gets her hopes up.

"I've been working on a sketch of Z," he blurted out. *Holy shit, Batman. Why did you tell her that? All you've got is something even Fred thinks is a creepy stalker picture.*

"Really? You took the time to do that?" He could practically hear her smiling.

"Of course." *Because what other romantic gesture is there besides drawing a half-naked superhero version of you with giant tits?*

Get it together, Don Juan. She doesn't want you like that. He ate a last forkful of vegetables and broken noodles.

"See you soon?"

"Yup." *Why has every day since I met her been the best and worst day of my life?*

"Okay, bye, Greg!"

"Bye, Zarah."

"So?" Fred asked, stepping back into the living room, still in mock surrender.

"She's excited."

A wolfish grin spread across Fred's face. "Bet she is."

"But, like, what am I supposed to do?"

"Like Bastian told you before, just be yourself. She

knows what you are and only ran away twice so far." He sat down next to him. "Someone in this apartment should be happy."

Greg took a deep breath. "All right, then. Wish me luck."

"Why don't you bring her over here?" said Fred, his gray eyes now seeming less bloodshot and more calculating.

Greg raised an eyebrow.

"I mean, fuck, I know why you don't want to," Fred said, gesturing to his orange-smeared undershirt.

"No, no," said Greg, "I do want her to meet you guys. Eventually. She just, like, almost got an anxiety attack going to the candy store yesterday on our one-and-only date."

Fred nodded knowingly. "So if she meets Bastian and me...."

"If she runs a third time, it's probably over."

Fred thought for a moment. "Didn't you say she lives above the abandoned sushi buffet where that annoying guy plays guitar on Saturday nights?"

"Yeah."

Fred's eyes lit up to full-on scheming mode.

Greg frowned. "Whatever plan you're concocting, flush it down the toilet."

Fred shrugged innocently. "I have no idea what you are talking about."

"Ugh, nevermind, just let me grab my sketchbook and meet my doom." Greg stood up from the couch and stared down at Fred's greasy hair. "And, like, bathe or something while I'm gone. You look like Splinter kicked you out of the sewer because you smelled too bad."

"Bathe on my night off?" Fred smiled and shooed him out of the living room. "Go on, grab your 'concept art' and get outta here. Oh, and good fucking luck."

CHAPTER 12

As Greg walked in the cool Colorado summer evening light toward Zarah's apartment, his head swayed to Elton John's "Levon," the song that had reconnected his parents years after their first meeting. Greg hummed and waded through a group of smokers outside Lark Tavern, thinking about how his basis for true love seemed like the start of a bad joke. *Did you hear the one about the deacon and the nun who fell in love over a gay man's song about a balloon salesman who blasphemously named his son Jesus?*

But perhaps the punchline was that it just worked. He remembered what they'd said to him when he'd been turned down by three girls for prom, just before Eve Myers asked him out of the blue. The third no, Stacey Mills, was the hardest. The first two had the decency to lie and say they were just going with a group of friends. But Stacey had just laughed.

"Sit down, son," his father had said, peering over his bifocals and patting a spot next to him on the long leather couch. His dad wasn't a bad-looking guy, and age seemed to have improved him from the goofy, skinny white kid Greg had glimpsed once in an old photo album. He had a full head of wavy salt-and-pepper hair and a square jaw, the latter of which Greg hoped would come to him soon. Greg's mom sat nestled next to her husband, her black hair framing the high cheekbones of her dark brown face in curly springs.

"Love is God's greatest gift," his dad began in his deacon orator's voice as Greg sat next to him.

Greg picked at his fingernails. "Then why did God make me, uh, repulsive to all womankind?"

"You are no such thing," said his mom, gripping Greg's hand with both of hers.

"But I am." He stood and gestured to himself. "I'm skinnier than Becca Summers, and she's going to nationals for cross-country."

"Your mother taught me something, son, when I met her the second time." His dad patted his mom's shoulder.

"What, that we Normands only have a chance with a woman if she's drunk?"

"Greggie!"

"No," his dad said, then took a slow breath. "What is God's second greatest commandment?"

"Love thy neighbor as thyself," recited Greg.

"Yes," said his dad, leaning forward and adjusting his bifocals. "Which presupposes that you love yourself." *And here comes the sermon.* "Think about that: God calls us to love ourselves. And when I first met your mother," he paused to shoot her a look, "I was so immersed in my work that I hadn't taken the time to love myself. I wasn't until later that I did, and then God chanced us to meet again."

"He's right," said Greg's mom, her amber eyes soft as if to accept Greg's pain as her own. "It never gets easier just because you have someone else. You need to be ready to take on the universe alone before it's hand-in-hand with the right someone."

I should call them, Greg thought as he stopped in front of Finn's Tattoos, where Finn the Boston terrier stood guard, snuffling on the stoop as usual. Greg was just steps away from Zarah's apartment building. Finn wagged his nubbin of a tail and trotted toward Greg to lick his hand.

"What if loving myself isn't enough, Finn?" He stared down the alleyway. "What if serious doomsday awaits me in apartment H, inexplicably located next to apartment M like a lost circle of hell?"

As he spoke, Elton John's "Levon" shifted to the banjo, tambourine, and harmonic vocals of Red Clover Ghost's "Dark Haired Queen."

As the song played, he imagined Zarah sitting at her desk, hair up in a bun with a few defiant ringlets draping over her thin shoulder, as she fed X the hamster seed-by-seed. Her makeup-less face showed freckles across her cheeks, freckles he knew she thought he didn't notice. And then X squeaked, and she treated him with a circus sprinkle, grinning at the memory of yesterday's date to Kaleido Kandy. He could just almost smell the pear scent of her hair.

He came back to reality as Finn pawed impatiently at his hand. Greg scratched the dog's ears. "I'm losing my mind over this girl, Finn. I shouldn't be listening to this song, this playlist."

He stared toward the rusting metal stairs leading up to her apartment.

"Time to face my doom, huh?" he said as he gave the dog one last pat. Greg took a deep breath and let the courage of the music fill him. "Oh, my *red* haired queen," he started to sing, changing the words of the folk tune. "Prettiest face that I have ever seen."

With each step, he gained speed, until he was bounding up the alleyway's rusting metal stairs and knocking on Zarah's brown, chipped door, which opened to reveal Zarah's smiling face. Her hair was indeed up in a bun with a few flyaways, freckles highlighting her cheekbones.

He pulled out his ear buds and placed them in his shoulder bag. *She's smiling. Smiling is good. Say something.* "Hey!" he greeted a little too enthusiastically.

"So," she said, practically bouncing, "come in and

show me your concept art!"

"Oh, that." *Great. Just great. You'll definitely think a borderline pornographic cartoon of you is worthy of your current excitement.* He patted his shoulder bag. "It's not really that good."

Faster than he could react, she reached for his bag, slipped it off his shoulder, and deftly maneuvered through her obstacle course of furniture to her bed with all the nimbleness of Catwoman. "It's like Christmas," she said with a grin as she sat down.

"Now, wait," he said, making his way toward her. "It won't make sense unless I explain it first."

She pulled out his sketchbook and set it on her lap. "Okay, I'm waiting."

He reached her bed and flopped down next to her. "Now give me that," he said, leaning in and reaching for the sketchbook.

She pulled it away. "I want to turn the pages."

"Fine. Just, okay, so the first one is of—"

"Graham crackers," she whispered as she flipped back the front cover to reveal Greg's drawing of a faceless Jude.

"Yeah, it's not done yet...."

"It's incredible," she said, running her fingers over Jude's gold wings.

"Really?" Watching her fingertips gently trace his unfinished art, Greg couldn't help but grin. He wanted to hug her, to gently tuck her loose curls back into her bun, to kiss her freckled nose because she loved what he'd created—faceless and all.

"I think I like him like this," she said, circling Jude's empty face with her pointer finger. "It's as if his visage is too sacred for mortals to see."

"I guess I never thought about it like that."

She flipped past Jude through Greg's drawings of the Universe, the heavenly City of Jerusalem, and Purgatory USA, stopping just before a scantily-clad Z. "I can't believe it," she whispered, paging back to Jude. She looked up and locked eyes with Greg. "I don't even know if I want to see Z now."

Halleluiah! "Really? Why not?"

She turned and reached for one of her stick-figure Zs pinned to the wall and laid it down on the page next to Jude. "Because mine looks so stupid," she mumbled.

Nothing about you could ever be stupid. "Nonsense," he said, picking up her drawing. "Dee-dee-dum—dum—dee-dee-dum-dah-dummmm," he sang as he pretended the drawing was flying through the air.

She broke into a chuckle. "What are you doing?"

"Um, you mean what is Z doing," he corrected. "Dee-dee-dum—dum—dee-dee-dum-dah-dummmm.   She's flying to her theme song, of course."

"Theme song?"

"Obviously, every superhero has a theme song. 'Na-na-na-na-na-na-na-na-na-na Batman!'" he sang. "Just listen to the music in your head."

She bit her lip.

"Try this," he said, continuing to make Z fly. "What do you hear right now? Just hum it."

"I don't...hear...anything."

He made Z fall out of the air and land with a "Ka-blam!" on his sketch of Jude. "How can you not hear anything? Don't you ever sing to yourself?"

"No."

"Don't you ever listen to music and think, 'Wow, this should so be my theme song'? Like, mine is definitely Elton John's 'Rocket Man.'" He mimed holding a microphone and began to sing.

Zarah shook her head. "I don't listen to music."

Doesn't...listen...to...dear God. "What about the Chordinator?" he asked in desperation.

"The bane of my existence."

"Ouch. Wow. This is horrible. Because, like, music is pretty much the center of my universe." *A playlist for the doctor's office, a playlist for work, a playlist for sketching, for sleeping, for going to see Zarah-who-I-just-met-a-few-days-ago.*

She shrugged.

He shook his head. "You'll find your song, Zarah Smith. But for now, Z can borrow Europe's 'The Fiiii-nal Count-dowwwwwn!" He stood and sang the title as he flew Zarah's stick figure Z through the air again. "Dee-dee-dum—dum—dee-dee-dum-dah-dummmm!"

"Okay, okay," she said laughing, "maybe I'm ready to see your sketch of Z now." She began paging through his sketchbook again.

"No!" he shouted, letting stick-figure Z drop like a leaf to the floor as he snatched his sketchbook out of Zarah's hands. At the sight of her widened eyes, he hugged the sketchbook to his chest and rocked back and forth on his heels. "I mean, it doesn't do her justice. I don't know enough about her yet."

"Well," she said, her face relaxing slightly, "I told you she's an alien."

"So is TIX. And She-Ra and Superman and, well, Allen the Alien. You're giving me nothing, my dear."

"Moment of greatness," she mumbled. The atmosphere of the room shifted, as if a trigger had sent her into a trance. She pulled her knees to her chest and rubbed her Saint Christopher between her thumb and forefinger, all the while staring at nothing. In the still, silent air, even X the hamster stopped nibbling and scratching.

Shit, what just happened? What did I say? He sat back down next to her, but she remained rigid, no eye contact. "Look," he said, "I thought TIX was a waste until you described how you see him. If you could tell me what makes Z the incredible hero you know her to be, it would help me really capture her."

"She…she was disguised as an intern," Zarah said slowly, methodically, still gazing into dead air. "In a museum on Earth. After her planet was destroyed in a fire."

Greg leaned forward. "How'd she get to Earth?"

"There was a shooter in the museum," she continued without breaking. "No one knows why, but he wanted to kill everyone there with his shotgun. But he didn't. Because Z didn't let him. She hit him with the lightning from her hair and destroyed him. Because everyone on her planet had died except her, and she didn't want that to happen ever again."

As she told Z's story, Greg recalled glimpses of headlines, security footage of a masked shooter in a DC museum two years ago, and—suddenly—distinctly—the front-page photograph of a curly-haired redhead sobbing into a police officer's stomach.

No.

"Everyone was safe," she said emphatically, now rubbing furiously on her Saint Christopher medal. "No casualties."

Fourteen People Killed in DC Museum. Another Mass Shooting Hits the US. WHY? The headlines now rolled clearly through his memory.

She looked at him pleadingly. "Does that help? Could you draw someone like that?"

He sat in the moment, meeting her eyes, feeling her secret fill the space between them. Did she realize what she'd just told him? Did she—her innocent eyes pleaded harder—did she believe the story? But the redhead in the newspaper couldn't have been her, could it?

"I don't know if anyone could do Z justice," Greg whispered, fighting back unbidden tears. *Do not cry in front of her. And for the love of God, don't ask her. Not yet.*

"I know you can draw her," she said, nodding. Gently, she tucked her medal back into her shirt and released her knees. "Could you try?"

"I think I love you," he whispered, reaching to hug her. *Wait, what?* Time stopped and the moment hung with him reaching his arms around Zarah, though not yet touching her. *I can't love her. Not yet. I barely know her.* He breathed in the scent of her shampoo, and the moment continued as he wrapped his arms tight around her thin shoulders, face pressed into her hair. Gently, he kissed her curls.

She turned her head and nudged his face until her lips found his. She kissed him, hard. His sketchbook crashed to the floor and X let out a high-pitched squeak as she reached her hands under his shirt and onto his stomach, all the while thrusting her tongue into his mouth. Her warm palms ran over his chest and to his shoulders, where she dug in her nails and pulled him down on top of her.

His heart thudded against his chest and he kissed her back, wanting to take all her pain, wanting to feel her—

She unzipped his pants.

It's happening! Holy shit, why? What the hell am I supposed to do? He reached for her gym shorts and began to pull on them.

"Wait," she said, pulling away and gasping for breath. "I'm…I'm not ready." She looked up at him with watery eyes.

His heart continued to thud, his pulse beating hard now, too, against his jeans. "That's okay," he said, taking a deep breath and kissing her forehead. "That's okay." He took another breath and sat up slowly. Resting his head in his hands, he massaged his temples, inhaling and exhaling deliberately to calm his heart. *Ohmygod. Did she just unwittingly tell me the most significant and violent thing that ever happened to her, so naturally my response was to tell her I LOVED HER even though I JUST MET HER, and then she tried to have sex with me but changed her mind, and never said she loved me back, BECAUSE OBVIOUSLY, WHY WOULD SHE SAY THAT?*

What the hell am I doing? Why the hell did I say that?

"It's just been a couple years," she said, readjusting her shorts.

"Have you eaten dinner?" he asked as he zipped up his fly, hoping changing the subject would make her forget the whole thing.

"Oh." She blinked. "No, but my groceries get delivered

on Saturdays, so I planned on subsisting off pita chips and hummus until tomorrow."

Grocery deliveries. He smiled and returned to the moment, to quirky Zarah, to her somehow charmingly TIX-infested apartment. "So I take it you ate all the cake already?"

She laughed and shook her head. "Just half."

"Half? Zarah Smith, where the hell do you put all those calories?"

"Same place you do," she said, tousling his hair.

As he looked at her grinning expression, he wondered if they really, truly had a shot. The miracle baby with the bad ticker and the madcap woman with the doctored memory, taking on the world hand-in-hand. He could see the sketch in his mind, the brilliant ink of her red curls, the yellow light surrounding their hands, as they stood on the edge of the Earth, facing the Universe.

CHAPTER 13

"And so I..." Zarah trailed off and bit her lip, cheeks beginning to redden beneath her freckles.

"You what?"

She winced and buried her face in her hands. "It's too embarrassing."

Iris reached out and gently pulled Zarah's hands away from her face. "Then tell me so we can laugh about it," she said with a smile that creased the corners of her eyes.

"I..." Zarah looked away from Iris's hazel eyes and glanced around at the shelves of stone tablets, clay pots, eating utensils, jewelry, figurines, and other preserved artifacts inside the Babylonian storage closet. "I made out with him," she admitted.

"Old news. Give me the real story."

Even without looking, Zarah knew Iris's right eyebrow was raised as high as her grin was stretched wide. A childless divorcee in her forties, Iris often danced between playing both the mother and sister Zarah never had.

Zarah sighed, still avoiding eye contact. "I also pulled him down on top of me and tried to take his pants of," she whispered quickly.

"Wow."

"And then I made him stop," she said at normal volume, returning her gaze to Iris's knowing eyes. "I don't know what came

103

over me."

"You mean they don't teach that in school anymore?" Iris said with a laugh.

Zarah fiddled with her curls. "I just haven't…been with anyone in over two years. Not since Behnam."

"This Greg must be pretty cute, then?"

Zarah grinned and scrunched up her nose. "Adorable. He's got this mess of hair and these big thick green glasses and arms as skinny as mine." As she mentioned each feature, she gestured to her own in comparison.

"So nothing like Behnam?"

"No," Zarah said, remembering Behnam's well-defined arms, his confident stride, his wolfish grin that even in memory still taunted her to kiss him. Behnam sang flawless tenor and bari-tenor, swam a mile a day, and rode a Suzuki GSX-R.

To fuck him again would be fantastic.

But he wouldn't love the new Zarah, broken like an overused guitar string. He'd try. He'd try to be patient and faithful. He'd play his music only when she wasn't around, all the while wracking his brain for a clean way to be free.

Then there was Greg. Skinny, awkward, and more likely to ride a unicycle than a motorcycle. But he knew full-well what a mess she was. He knew about Z and about the grocery deliveries and her panic on Main Street. And he'd still said he loved her.

"What I want to know is, did you tell him?" asked Iris with raised eyebrows.

"Tell him what?"

"That you love him too, of course," she said with a little laugh, rubbing Zarah's arm like a mother would.

"No," she mumbled, looking at the linoleum floor. Of course she hadn't. She couldn't love him. She couldn't love. Not since…

"But you think you do, or that you could," prodded Iris.

She pictured Greg in her mind, how frail he'd looked sitting up on the exam room table. He didn't have the arms or the walk or the grin, or the voice or the athlete's body or the daredevil nature. But he had the hair. The glasses. The amber eyes. The nervous rocking. The carefully-sketched angel wings and awesome cityscapes. When he'd held her hand, when he'd told her he loved her...the overpowering surge of energy, of joy, of—she didn't even know—exploding from her heart had pulled her to him, had begged—needed—her to be with him, to have him.

"Afterward," Zarah continued her story, "he ate hummus with me for dinner because I'm too neurotic to go to the grocery store. Then he sat down next to me on the bed and sketched out Z before my eyes." She remembered the carefully-shaded ringlets, the faint stippling of freckles, even the hint of pain beneath her dark, masked eyes. "It was just in pencil," she continued, "but it was practically a photograph of her. Then we fed X some sprinkles. He's coming over to make me dinner tomorrow." Zarah shook her head and looked at the floor. "Do you think he could really love me?"

But when she looked up, Iris was gone. The shelves of artifacts were now posters of the Indomitable X hanging on the exposed brick walls of her apartment. On the kitchenette counter sat an empty hummus container from Greg's visit an hour before. Zarah's thumb and forefinger were rubbing furiously at Iris's Saint Christopher medal as she sat on the edge of her bed. Iris had always taken it with her into the closet, to help her find things. Until—

Outside, a guitar strummed gently.

Not now, Chordinator. Go the fuck away.

He strummed again, more loudly.

Zarah tucked Iris's medal back into her shirt and stepped toward her desk for her ear plugs. But as she glanced out the dark window and down onto the sidewalk, she realized it wasn't the Chordinator at all.

It was Behnam.

Scrambling, she leaned as far as she could over X's cage, barely on her tiptoes, pressing her nose against the window. Her heart thudded in her chest, through her fingertips, her face. Under the street light, Behnam Shirazi was unmistakable—his thick black hair, his wide shoulders, the way he cradled the guitar in his—

No, wait. Behnam was left-handed. He was studying law in LA, not performing on the streets on Lark Springs.

The man's hair lightened from black to brown; his shoulders drooped. He strummed another chord with his right hand.

She backed away from the window and slumped into her red desk chair. This was exactly why she didn't listen to music anymore. It sent her places. It always had. Only now, it sent her to haunted catacombs, facing ghosts still begging to be buried in their sarcophagi, screaming, pleading to be beheld and laid to rest. No longer did music take her to caterpillar racetracks to the moon, to her future with Behnam and a herd of children, to catacombs ripe for excavation with a promise of mystery and treasure.

And then the words came. The lyrics of U2's "Where the Streets Have no Name" flooded from the man on the street, only in Behnam's powerful bari-tenor and Zarah's strums of the guitar.

The foot-and-incense-and-ramen-and-pot smell of the college dorm room hallway surrounded her, the white walls, the matted and stained carpet. Behnam's face, eyes closed, singing each word deliberately with a pained look.

She'd known this song was about a city in Africa, somewhere maybe she and Behnam would go with the Peace Corps after graduating. But she'd always thought it sounded like the loneliest song in the world, someone who at once wanted anonymity and community, who wanted to—

And suddenly, the scene changed. Behnam stood on the edge of his bed in his dorm room, walls covered with posters from *The Lion King's* 1997 debut on Broadway, *Rent*, *Wicked*, and now Boulder's upcoming student production of *Les Misérables*. Below Behnam, Zarah sat cross-legged on his green area rug, plucking the strings of her guitar. It was the day before *Les Mis* opened and the first time she'd heard him sing Marius's solo, "Empty Chairs at Empty Tables," in its entirety.

Acting as Marius, Behnam surveyed his dorm room as if gazing at individual ghosts of the friends he'd just lost in battle at the barricade. He nearly whispered the words, face drawn, voice cracking with heartbreak.

"No," Zarah said aloud, trying to pull herself back to the present. The music stopped. The posters changed from Broadway to the Indomitable X, Behnam's rug to her desk chair.

She stood again to peer over X's cage and out her window. Behn—the Chordinator—whoever—was gone, or had never been there in the first place.

She sighed and reached for X's sunflower seeds, which she began to feed him through the bars of his cage. He squeaked his approval.

"Behnam's not here," she said to the hamster. "He's in LA. Or somewhere." She gazed around her room, re-familiarizing herself. "We're not in a dorm room. We're not in a museum closet. We're home." As she scanned her posters, her eyes landed on Greg's pencil masterpiece, now pinned next to her stick figure scribbles by her bed. Z stared back at her with the slightest of smiles, as if she knew all along Zarah would realize her mistake, as if only she knew what was real on this mess of a planet.

Zarah turned back to her hamster and unlatched the door on the front of his cage. The little gray-blue hamster pawed forward into Zarah's cupped hands and blinked at her with black beady eyes. With one finger, Zarah gently pet X's warm, soft fur.

Without thinking, she began to sing to him in a whisper.

Little Catty Caterpillar
Just had to win that race
But the only way to win,
She thought with a grin,
Is if the track's built to that place
Where nobody's been:
I'll build a racetrack to the moon!

X began to scamper out of her hands, and she fumbled with him until she set him back in his cage. She gazed around the room again, and it hadn't changed this time. No ghosts. No catacombs.

She smiled at her hamster. "Okay then, mister," she said in a voice that sounded to her the tiniest bit like the old Zarah. "No more music tonight."

CHAPTER 14

Greg descended the rusting metal stairs of Zarah's building and turned to blink back up toward her lit apartment. He buttoned his flannel against the nighttime summer Colorado breeze, which held a twinge of cold akin to a Texas November chill. Lark Springs seemed wholly asleep now at 10 PM, save for a few lit windows like Zarah's and the persistent street lamp sentinels lining Main Street.

He recalled her unsettlingly-composed face, the metronome-driven cadence she'd used to tell Z's story, the way she'd snapped back to quirky Zarah as if out of hypnosis. Would she be okay without him tonight? Alone with nothing but a hamster and TIX posters to keep her company?

Cool it, Don Juan, he thought. *You're not a superhero, and that shooting happened over two years ago. Stop trying to rescue her.*

He pulled his phone out of the pocket of his jeans, where Red Clover Ghost's "Dark Haired Queen" remained paused from hours earlier. But music just didn't feel right. Not now. All he could think about was the way she'd told that story. He entered a search for "DC Smithsonian shooting," and instantly, his phone bombarded him with distant-but-familiar photos: police tape, flashing lights, one sole officer carrying a gun with a look of determination. The stuff of a great comic.

But then the fourteen obituary photos. A now-fatherless child playing basketball alone in his driveway. And, *There!*—Greg's body tightened with recognition—the iconic curly-haired redhead sobbing into a police officer's stomach.

Greg zoomed in on the photo, trying unsuccessfully to catch a glimpse of her face shielded by a cloak of hair.

He'd always been drawn to this picture, the grip of her hands, the way her leg muscles slackened as if about to buckle. He'd wondered who this woman was, what she had witnessed, whom she had lost. Wondered if anyone besides that police officer had offered her comfort.

The caption simply read: "Survivor mourns."

He looked back up at Zarah's window. Was that why he'd said he loved her? Because she was that very image come to life, still needing someone to cling to? Because he wanted to be Jude and watch over her in all her hopelessness? Was that even love?

Maybe the picture wasn't her, after all. Maybe she didn't need anyone's help, least of all his. Maybe what she needed most was to be left the hell alone.

He needed Bastian. Or his parents. Or anyone, except maybe Fred. There just wasn't a playlist for *Thinking You Might Be in Love with Someone You're Not Even Sure You're Dating Who Repressed a Memory of a Horribly Violent Event and Probably Should See a Licensed Therapist, but You're Just Not Fucking Equipped to Handle This Since You Keep Putting off Seeing a Damned Heart Doctor Yourself, You Idiot.*

What if he went back up? Her apartment window was still lit. Had too much time passed? Would she let him back in?

His phone vibrated wildly in his hand and blasted the all-time Wilford favorite, "I've Got Friends in Low Places." *Fred.*

Greg scrambled to answer the phone as it shattered the

quiet of the night.

"What do you need, Fred?" he asked with a twinge of exasperation.

"Put your pants back on, because Bastian and I are on the way with a shit-ton of pizzas. We're kidnapping you and the Z girl and forcing you to introduce her before you 'Greg it up' too much."

Greg groaned. "Not now, Fred."

"But it's Tony's pizza."

Tony's. Greg could almost smell the putrid, mouth-watering aroma of Tony's pizza covered in little pepperoni bowls of grease. His stomach growled despite himself, still empty from the meager meal of hummus, chips, and cake.

"Oh, and I bathed," said Fred. "And shaved. I'm even wearing a shirt with buttons."

Greg continued to stare at Zarah's window. No, he couldn't ask that of her. She needed time alone. "Well, I think you probably just saved me from 'Gregging it up' even more than I already have. Pick me at Main and 6th. I could use some pizza." He paused, then added, "And whiskey."

A half hour later, Greg leaned forward on their tattered sofa and downed his seventh shot of Jack. The burning warmed his chest and inflicted just enough pain that he forgot for a moment about love and not love, shootings and palpitations. But then his chest cooled and the pain softened to a warm tingle.

"I told her I loved her," he said, staring straight ahead to avoid eye contact with his roommates sitting on either side of him.

Both Fred and Bastian groaned.

"Greggie, why? That's a terrible idea."

"A fucking stupid idea."

Greg continued to stare ahead toward their makeshift plywood coffee table, where four untouched, steaming, grease-soaked Tony's pizzas taunted him with their pepperoni-and-cheese taste lingering on the air. But every time he thought about grabbing and devouring a slice, his stomach sickened at the image of that newspaper photo, now overlaid with Zarah's incongruously calm face as she'd told her story.

"I don't know why. The words just, like, came out." He shook his head. "And then she was all over me, pulling my clothes off and stuff." His face flushed at the memory, his pulse deepened in his groin as he could almost feel her hands running up and down his chest, down to his jeans. "But then she stopped. She said she wanted to wait. So we ate hummus and cake."

If Fred or Bastian responded, Greg couldn't hear them. All seven shots careened into his brain at once, sloshing around and muddling it, pulling him back to Zarah, her warm parted lips, her hands—oh God, if she'd just kept going! The room tilted like a roller coaster before the first drop.

"I'd better pass out before I start throwing up," he announced, lifting himself from the sofa. "But thanks. I needed this."

At six o'clock the next morning, Greg sat cross-legged on his bed, shading a fold in one of Z's flowing curls with red colored pencil. Her hair draped over most of her face and down her shoulder as she clung white-knuckled to the brown sackcloth robes of a faceless man. From the man's back sprouted gold, intricately feathered wings, and his head tilted down toward Z's, as if about to kiss her hair.

A knock at the door interrupted Greg's sketching and reawakened his throbbing whiskey headache.

Another knock, this one reverberating through his brain. "Open up, Greggie," came Bastian's voice from the other side.

"Fine," moaned Greg, closing his sketchbook. "Come in if you have to."

Bastian, dressed in a tee shirt for the weekend, peered

in as if he were scanning a haunted house for traps. His eyes finally rested on Greg and widened in mock surprise. "You're alive!" he exclaimed.

His voice pounded Greg's temples. "Barely," he mumbled as he scooted over on his bed to allow Bastian a seat. "Seven shots shouldn't do this to a man and then wake him up at this hour on a Saturday."

Bastian sat down next to Greg, eyebrow raised. "So about last night," he began.

"I drank it off," said Greg, longing to return to his sketch and eventually to sleep. "I'm good now."

Bastian furrowed his brows and narrowed his eyes as if trying to shoot X-ray vision through Greg's forehead and into his brain. "I don't buy it. Something else happened. Maybe you don't want to tell Fred, but I hope by now you can trust me."

Greg sighed as he felt his friend's brown eyes beaming through his pounding skull. Bastian had stayed in the closet through most of high school, even though he'd told Greg freshman year. It had been their secret until Bastian chose to share it himself three years later. If Greg could trust anyone now with Zarah's secret, it was the man who still called him Greggie.

Greg dug in his pocket for his phone and pulled up the photo of the redheaded woman. "This is from that DC museum shooting a couple years ago," he said as he handed it to Bastian. "There was something she said… I think she was there. I think this is her."

Bastian stared at the photo as if for the first time, as if the shooting had just happened a moment ago. "Shit, Greggie."

"I think she needs help," said Greg, scratching the back of his neck. "But the only thing I could think to do was hug her and tell her I loved her. And then she…"

"Jumped you?" Bastian said, looking back again at his friend matter-of-factly.

"Yeah."

"Did you mean it?"

"Mean what?"

Bastian smiled and shook his head. "That you love her."

Greg reconsidered the question he'd asked himself so many times last night. *Yes, I mean, no, of course not, I've only known her a few days.* "I don't know," he said after a moment. "I don't even know what to do, how to act. I don't even know for sure if this is her or if we're dating."

Bastian handed Greg's phone back to him. "Just be there for her, I guess. Shit, I don't know. Have you called her? Texted her?"

"Bastian, it's six AM."

His roommate broke into a grin. "Good call, Greggie, good call."

"But I'm supposed to go over after my shift tonight."

Bastian shrugged. "I wish I knew something to tell you. If you just do what Greggie would do, hell, you'll do better than Fred or I ever would. You'll work through it."

Greg smiled. "Thanks, man."

"You know who might be a better help?" Bastian asked, lips pursed in scheming thought. "There are these two people we know who've won pretty hard at marriage for a few decades."

Shit. I do need to call them. But— "What am I supposed to tell them? 'Hey, Mom and Dad, I don't even know if I'm dating this girl, but I think I might be in love with her, and also that she might need therapy'?"

"Well, if you're going to put it like that, you might as well ask Fred for advice."

Greg waved his hands in a shooing motion. "Get to work, Sage Sebastian, before you waste all your wisdom in one hopeless place."

"Nothing's wasted on you, my friend," Bastian said as he gripped his friend's shoulder and stood. "Good luck."

CHAPTER 15

Van Halen's "Panama" blasted over the speakers at Comics Inked. Saturday, the day of families with kids sharing fresh-smelling new comic books, the day of 80s hair metal on the local radio, the day of Greg's 12-hour shift. Were this any other Saturday, Greg would jump onto the checkout counter and play air guitar during customer lulls. But this was the day after seven shots of Jack, and in front of him on the counter was a nearly-complete portrait of Jude and Z.

As Greg hunched over the counter and shaded the curve of Z's neck, he thought about last night's almost-sex. The blurted proclamation of love. The nine times he'd clicked on her number but never hit "call." Because what if he'd imagined the whole thing? What if last night was just another drawing on his notepad, another set of panels in a comic that didn't exist?

Meanwhile, a normal Saturday continued around him. People still bought comics, asked if there were any more signed TIX comics (*how many did you think we had, people?*), browsed around the store without ever buying anything. All the while, Greg remained glued to the page, the story, the memory, the snapshot, the girl, her pear-smelling hair.

"Pretty busy, there." Val's gruff voice pulled Greg out of his thoughts and back into Comics Inked. Val was facing him in front of the checkout counter, hands on the countertop as if about to leap over for a fight scene. Eddie Van Halen rocked his solo over the speakers.

Greg tensed. "Um."

Val's eyebrows creased close together.

"I mean, well, it's just this thing."

"That tall blue-haired chick just asked you for another postmodern graphic novel suggestion, and you didn't even look up."

Greg blinked.

"Don't worry, I was fully capable of helping, and I'm glad you're working on your stuff, but the customers...." Val cocked his head to the side and stared at Greg's drawing, as if trying to see upside-down. "Seriously, you doing okay?"

Greg looked up at Val and then back down at his drawing, at Z's white knuckles, her dress crumpling as her legs buckled.

"It's for our comic," Greg lied.

Val straightened but continued to stare at the drawing, face drawn as if he'd just overheard a terrible secret.

"You look like shit," said Val. "Take the rest of the day."

A phone call later, Greg headed to Zarah's apartment early. He pressed his ear buds into his ears, but only silence came out of them. There just wasn't a playlist for how he felt, and hadn't been since last night.

Bastian had told him to just "do what Greggie would do," but what did that even mean?

Was it a mistake to tell Bastian? Because Zarah doesn't even know what had happened to her, right? Does she realize she told a complete fantasy?

What happens when she realizes?

What happens if she never does?

Greg yanked out his ear buds. *Fuck the silence. I'm tired of thinking.*

Instead, he listened to the evening around him, alive with its own soundtrack of skateboard and stroller wheels against pavement, people laughing and talking, forks clinking against plates on restaurant patios.

As he passed the Greek restaurant decorated with canopies and carnival lights and smelling strongly of fresh baba ghanoush, he thought about calling Zarah and having her meet him for dinner.

No, Don Juan, he corrected himself. *She's afraid of walking. Of people. Better stick to the plan and cook something from her grocery shipment.*

And then it caught his eye: *Kris the Sad Rhinoceros.*

In the peaked display window of an old-stone-church-turned-coffee-shop stood an array of books. In the center, outlined in bold black like a classic cartoon, was an indigo rhinoceros with a perfect parabola of a frown.

Being a heart patient and thereby an avid avoider of most forms of caffeine, Greg had never been inside Mountain City Coffee House, as the sign read in calligraphy. Its fresh smell had always called to him, reminding him of Sunday mornings at home when Mom fixed a pot of coffee while Dad cooked eggs Benedict and grilled asparagus.

He continued to stare at the book in the window. *Doesn't Zarah call her boss something like that? The Rhinocer....Rhinocerkris! Yes!*

The door jingled as he walked inside.

He was greeted with a stronger aroma of coffee and hazelnut, charming folk guitar, and an entire shelf of *Kris the Sad Rhinoceros* right next to the door. He picked up one of the books and opened the cover.

Suddenly, he felt like he had sprinted up seven flights of stairs. He nearly dropped the book as he fumbled for a seat at an empty table.

Sitting down, he rubbed his chest and breathed deeply.

Go away, he willed it. He swallowed and breathed rhythmically to the live guitar.

Pretend, he told himself. *Pretend you're fine.*

He reached to open the book, but a stone fist seemed to reach inside his chest and grip his heart and lungs.

He doubled over and gasped.

"Are you okay."

The voice was monotone and devoid of any emotion, even the inflection of forming a question.

"Drink."

A water bottle wavered in his immediate vision, a disembodied hand placing it on the table. The hand removed the bottle's cap and scooted the water closer, next to *Kris the Sad Rhinoceros*.

Greg reached for the bottle but felt the table lurch forward. His chest continued to pound. Water wouldn't help. It never helped. He shifted his focus from the bottle to the children's book in front of him, the cartoon rhinoceros's face twisted like a funhouse mirror.

"Don't worry. I'm calling 9-1-1."

"No," spat Greg with what breath he had left. *No? What the fuck is wrong with me? I'm going to die in the damned bookstore, face-down on an unpurchased children's book.*

Something was crushing his chest.

The pounding.

He gulped at the air. Splotches of black.

"Your heart."

Greg looked up at the voice's source. Across from him sat a stranger with round bookworm reading glasses, a gray shirt with giant cat eyes and whiskers, and pale pink lips drawn into an expressionless line. The world continued to twist and skew around this woman, who neither smiled nor frowned, neither wrinkled an eyebrow in concern nor raised it in fear, but bored intently into Greg's eyes as if her glasses granted x-ray vision.

"It…it happens sometimes," explained Greg. The stone hand inside his chest slackened. He breathed deeply.

The world settled.

"Your book," said the stranger, pointing to the children's book with an unmoving gaze still locked onto Greg's soul.

Greg rubbed his temples and nodded at the book.

"It's signed."

Greg blinked. *Oh God, I've died. I've died, and now I'm in small-talk purgatory.*

The stranger stood and, hands in her pockets, walked away.

Greg pressed his hand to his chest. Were he in a comic book, he'd chase after the stranger. But his chest, the exhaustion. This was the worst one since the hospital, the worst one that hadn't taken him under.

Instead of chasing the stranger, the angel with an expressionless face, he took a sip from the water bottle.

CHAPTER 16

Zarah scurried around the kitchenette, hair swept back in a light blue handkerchief, humming to herself as she alternated between checking on the oven and whipping icing. The smell of chocolate cake permeated her apartment. Beneath her feet, X frolicked in his hamster ball.

"No judgment, X," she said, breaking her humming. "It's been an hour, he hasn't called, and damn it, I feel like eating something." X squeaked as his ball bounced off a cabinet.

"I know, it's terribly cliché. And just because he hasn't called doesn't mean he's not coming." She checked on the cake again, beginning to crisp on the corners and sides. "But what if he isn't? Last night, I tried to tear off his clothes, and then said never mind and offered him hummus and chips." She pulled the cake out and rested it on a cooling rack. "Hummus and chips. That's not even a real meal."

She looked down at her yellow tank top, dusted with flour and cocoa powder. She could only imagine what her face must look like. Maybe he wasn't coming, but she stepped into the bathroom anyway to at least splash off any stray flour.

"Hummus and chips," she continued to mutter to herself as she patted her face dry. As she hung up her towel, she looked once more at herself in the mirror. The way her hair was carelessly swept back, the way her freckles were darker from the summer sun, that light blue handkerchief she'd bought at some old lady's yard sale in Boulder—it all painted a perfect picture of college Zarah.

College Zarah played guitar in the dorm hallways, made up songs about caterpillars and rainbows, and wouldn't binge-eat fucking cake alone with her hamster over some boy not calling.

She'd sing about it.

Zarah slouched her posture as if she were leaning against a dorm wall. She sang:

> *We'll build a racetrack to the moon*
> *Gonna get there soon*
> *We'll build a racetrack to the moon with our best friends*

She held her hands up as if cradling her polished pawn shop Fender.

> *We'll build a racetrack to the moon*
> *And sing this little tune*

But that guitar was interred in its case under her bed. Dead, like her life before—

A knock at the door interrupted her thoughts.

Greg! "Thank goodness, X. That was going down a weird, dark, Saturday-night-in-with-an-entire-pity-cake path." She stepped over X in his hamster ball as she moved toward the door.

She opened it door expecting to find a fidgety, bouncing Greg with artwork under his arm.

But he was sunken, like he'd been awake for days although she knew he hadn't. His face was drawn and clammy, his eyelids heavy, his hair haggard, his body inert.

Had he been sleepless thinking about last night? Thinking and thinking about how she was too neurotic after all and had to break it off?

Wait, why did her mind go there? It wasn't all about her. But, *graham crackers*, she was genuinely starting to fall for him and—

"You don't look well," she finally said.

A slight smile tugged at the corners of his lips as he stepped through the doorway. "Well, you look delightful," he said, short of breath, as if he'd spent the entire day moving sofas. "Your hair looks nice like that. Very Z."

Zarah patted at her mane. "Z's got ringlets. I've got—"

"Can I sit down?"

"Sure." She took his arm. It was shaking. This wasn't a breakup. "You're not okay, are you?"

"I'd prefer to lie to you," he said as he sat on her bed. "But I won't. I'm okay now. But I wasn't earlier."

The cold sweat, the fatigue, the shortness of breath. Why didn't she see it before? They were all tell-tale signs of—

She knew she should call 9-1-1. She knew from every CPR class, every patient chart, every ounce of anything she'd learned at a cardiologist's office that she should call. Right now.

But this was Greg the 26-year-old, Greg the artist of X and angels and cityscapes, Greg who definitely couldn't be having a heart attack.

"These episodes come and go," he said.

Episodes? What episodes? Was he having one right now? She scrolled through diagnosis codes in her mind. "Greg, you need to see the doctor."

He shrugged.

"No, I'm serious. I've seen these symptoms before."

"I'm fine. I've always been fine."

"'Always been fine' isn't good enough. I just met you, and I don't want to lose you." As the words poured out of her heart, something inside her scrambled to retract them, to affirm that she couldn't feel that way, couldn't need someone, couldn't cope with them—

"Okay, okay!" He grabbed her hand. "I promise I'll call Monday."

"No, I'll set one up for you myself."

He held up his hands. "Go ahead. I'm afraid to stand in your way." He paused, and a light seemed to go off in his mind. "Oh, I almost forgot! I got you something." He reached into his messenger bag, still strapped across his body. "So a stranger helped me in the coffee shop. Gave me water. Calmed me down. Not super friendly, to be honest, but helpful to a dying person nonetheless—not that I'm dying! Because I'm not. But anyway, I thought maybe I'd seen an actual angel or something until the barista was all like, 'Oh my god, Morrow Maynard never talks to anyone!'" Greg paused and leaned in as if to whisper, but only talked louder and more quickly, sounding more like himself. "Remember I mentioned Morrow Maynard, author of *Can You Crack a Cookie*, resident famous person of Lark Springs, when we were on our walk? That's who helped me. And wrote and signed this book. Look!"

He pulled out a brightly-colored children's book and handed it to her. On the front cover was a purple rhinoceros with a big, thick black frown. The cartoon style reminded her of something she'd seen before somewhere, though not in a children's book. She couldn't quite place it.

Then she noticed the title. *Kris the Sad Rhinoceros.*

Couldn't be.

She looked up to meet Greg's amber eyes, bright and filled with energy now. "Like your boss, right?" he said. "I mean, that's why I picked it up for you in the first place. But, hey, here's the author, the one who helped me." He turned the book in Zarah's hands to the back cover, where Kris-with-glasses stared back at her.

The cat drawings in Kris's office. That's where she'd

seen the style before.

"Apparently, Morrow is pretty much mute and stays out of the public eye," Greg babbled, but his words faded as if underwater while Kris stared and stared back at her.

Always lurking. Always staring.

What did she see?

Zarah's stomach tightened. The air in the room seemed to strangle her.

She sees me.

She sees inside my head.

She knows.

She knows about Iris.

"Is…is there something wrong?"

Zarah looked up at Greg instead of the Rhinocerkris, in her apartment instead of the storage closet.

She released Iris's Saint Christopher medal she'd begun rubbing. "The author. The author is my boss."

Greg blinked. "Oh. Wow. That's, uh, that's weird."

Zarah nodded.

"But you don't actually call…"

"No, no. Not even around Franklin."

"So there's no way your boss knows the nickname."

Zarah shook her head.

"But you're still upset."

Upset didn't begin to measure it. Kris couldn't be omniscient, wasn't omniscient. Omniscience didn't exist outside of comic books and fantasy and mythology. But it was uncanny, the way Kris had started lurking ever since Zarah's internship, staring more and more intently.

"She knows something," she finally said. "She's always looking into my eyes like she can see my brain." She turned the book over in her hands. "Thank you, Greg. This was really thoughtful. I was just caught off-guard."

"No, no, I get it. Weird day." His face brightened. "Hey. About food." He started digging through his bag. "I figured I'd be, you know, too weak to make dinner after the whole mishap. So I brought these sandwiches from the coffee shop," he said, producing them like prizes, "which were on-the-house since I had an almost heart attack in their dining area."

Zarah grabbed a sandwich, and Greg tapped his against hers as if to "cheers."

"Next time," he said. "Next time, I'll bring on the culinary genius."

CHAPTER 17

Zarah clenched Greg's file as she stood in the doorway of the reception area the next morning. The open room was vaguely familiar—the low-hanging lantern-style lights, the lavender essential oil diffuser, the clackety-clack of keyboards, the incessant buzz of phone calls and patients and small talk. At the patient window sat Angie and Brock, twins whom Zarah had met once in passing since they started last year. Lina, the scheduler, sat in a corner with her back to Zarah. She talked into her headset in a sing-song-y voice, asking each caller to hold, pressing the buttons on the phone with startling fluidity. At the sound of her voice, memories washed over Zarah of having lunch together every Friday—often outside at a picnic table tucked under a tree— of talking about Monet and Picasso and Van Gogh, of sharing pudding recipes. As if nothing had changed in the past two years, Lina's favorite pink flowered sweater hung over her chair.

But everything had changed. That Zarah didn't exist anymore.

Zarah took a deep breath. *Time to become Z.*

Oxygen filled Zarah Smith's body, and as she exhaled, her lavender blouse and black skirt transformed into a yellow dress, her bun into loose ringlets, her freckles into a mask. But her red stilettos stayed the same.

Z crossed the room with head held high, approaching this human named Lina, who could help her schedule an appointment for the Great Gilgamesh.

Last night, Z had written her proposal out on paper with the intention of handing it to Lina and walking away. But upon second thoughts, and lengthy discussions with X, she'd determined that this approach would seem rather...inhuman. So, instead, she'd memorized the speech and delivered it in practice to X four times.

As Lina's call ended, Zarah tapped her on the shoulder.

Lina swiveled in her chair to reveal a large, round stomach.

Lina was pregnant?

When had that happened? Had there been a baby shower? When was she due? Boy or girl, and what was the name? Holy Marathon—she was huge!

Calm down.

"Lina," recited Z, *"Gregory Gilgamesh Normand would like to schedule a stress test as soon as possible. You see, he had an episode yesterday. I..."* She trailed off, and Z slipped away. Not only did the memory of Greg weak and short of breath terrify her, she realized she sounded absolutely ridiculous.

Lina smiled tentatively. Like usual, she had thick black bangs across her pale forehead. Her eye makeup today blended from yellow to orange to magenta and winged at the corners of her eyes. "Is that his file?" she asked.

"Yes," said Zarah, handing it to her.

Lina punched away on the keyboard and turned around with a frown. "I'm sorry, Zarah, it looks like we don't have an opening for three weeks."

Three weeks? But—

"Kris keeps a list of people to contact if we have cancellations. I don't have Mr. Normand listed as a priority, but maybe if you talk with her?"

Kris, the surly manager, the children's author, the good Samaritan who had tried to help Greg. Yes, talking would go swimmingly.

She nodded. "Thanks."

Zarah's brain told her to go, but she couldn't help but stare at Lina's swollen stomach. Zarah remembered Lina planning her destination wedding to Grand Canyon, scheming to open her own coffee shop one day where Zarah could make the cakes, growing a sleeve of flower tattoos, and deciding on names from *Gone With the Wind* to name all eight of her future children. The memories washed over her like towering waves, knocking her to her feet, clearing her lungs.

Somehow, Zarah had completely forgotten about this human being.

Her friend. From before.

"When are you due?" asked Zarah.

"Five weeks," Lina said with a shy grin, then whispered, "It's a girl."

"Scarlett?"

She beamed and nodded.

"That's beautiful," said Zarah.

When Zarah stepped into Kris's office, she didn't have a plan. She wasn't even Z.

What was she doing here?

Greg. She clung to his file like a talisman.

"Yes," Kris said in a tone that seemed more statement than inquiry, not looking up from her computer. The dark room reminded Zarah of a vampire's living room.

"Kris," Zarah forced herself to say, tightening her hands around the file and focusing on her breathing. What to say? This woman seemed impossible to communicate with. She constantly hovered and complained about Zarah working too slowly, but she'd given Zarah her job back with little notice. She'd helped Greg when he was in trouble. And she was a best-selling children's author.

The cats in the room seemed to scowl at her.

Kris looked up from her computer. "Yes."

"I..."

Kris sighed and started typing again on her laptop.

This wasn't going to work. She shouldn't have come here with no plan. Zarah's chest tightened and her hands started sweating and then what if her sweat bled into the file and got it so wet that no one could read the reports and then no one would ever know what was wrong with Greg and—

"Speak plainly, Zarah. You're obviously here for something. What do you need?

"Mr. Normand," said Zarah. "I'd...I'd like to put him on the waitlist for a stress test. You met him last night. In the coffee shop. He's really sick."

Kris nodded, and started typing on her laptop. "I'll add him. He should have gone to the hospital. Make him go next time."

Zarah nodded.

"I'd like a favor in return," said Kris, looking back up, lips pursed.

Marathon, here it comes.

"Lina will be out on maternity leave soon." Kris folded her hands in front of her. "Instead of hiring a temp, I will have you train with her to take her place. You will answer the phones and schedule patients. After she returns, I will consider Franklin's proposal to have you train as an EKG tech." Kris cleared her throat and began typing again. "Now, please leave my office. I'm very busy."

CHAPTER 18

Grab the paper. Grab the file. Open the prongs. Shove in the paper. Close the prongs.

Repeat.

It had been a week, but no cancellations for Greg to snag a stress test.

She still hadn't read the book—*Kris the Sad Rhinoceros.* Not wanting any more Kris in her life than she already had, she'd sent the book home with Greg.

She'd seen Greg nearly every day, whether to head to the candy store, stay in and sketch and read on the bed, or just talk. But, mercifully, he hadn't invited her to meet his roommates yet.

With plans looming for her to train with Lina next week, Zarah tried to savor the silence of her files, the smoothness of the paper, and the peace of her isolation.

"Isn't she lovely!" sang Franklin as he walked into the file room. He mimed handing a mic to Zarah.

"Um, no."

"It's Lina," he said, gently punching Zarah's shoulder. "She's at the hospital. Turns out the baby wants to make an entrance."

Graham crackers! Zarah's heart leapt in her chest. The

baby? Baby Scarlett? Zarah imagined Lina in her hospital gown, beaming and beautiful, holding tiny, swaddled Scarlett with scratches of black hair and big brown eyes. "Are we going to see her?"

"In labor? God, no!"

"I mean—"

"You're the new scheduler, remember? Congrats on your promotion."

No. Horror bubbled through the elation Zarah had just felt. "I—I can't," she sputtered. "The files."

"Come on. You can."

"But I didn't get training."

"Angie and Brock will help. Now go."

What else could she do? Defiantly file papers like a rogue robot?

Zarah placed one foot in front of the other and walked out of her filing area, across the hallway, and into the reception area where Angie and Brock sat with phones to their ears while checking in patients. Past their seats and their window to the waiting room was Lina's desk tucked away in a corner, flowered pink sweater still draped over her chair. Like a dreamer walking unwillingly toward danger, screaming futilely in her head for release from her corporeal prison, Zarah lowered herself into Lina's chair.

"Thank goodness you're here," said Angie next to her, light dancing off her bangled earrings. "We can't keep up. Damned phone lines are lit up like redneck Christmas."

Zarah stared at the blinking lights on her phone and wondered what would happen if she just refused to pick it up. Who exactly was on the other end in such desperate need of assistance? Bob Stedford with fettuccine or lasagna symptoms? Couldn't everyone just wait until tomorrow when Zarah would be back to filing papers?

Graham crackers in hell. Lina wouldn't be back for *months.*

The phone stopped ringing. This wasn't so bad.

Still…what if it was Greg? Or maybe it was someone like Greg, someone who needed help?

The phone rang again.

Zarah put on Lina's headset and pressed the Answer button. She breathed, mute.

"Hello? Is someone there?" said a man's voice.

Zarah began to bite the nails of her free hand, a habit she'd thought she'd kicked in middle school. "This…" she paused. She couldn't do it. He was a stranger.

"Yeah, miss?"

She breathed. Maybe Zarah couldn't do this, but Z could. The Others on her home planet believed she was a demon—and maybe she was—but she kept surviving.

And then she realized Z would never, ever answer phones in an office.

"This is…" she looked at Lina's memo pad next to the phone, which listed the office address, "…Lark Springs Cardiology."

"Oh. Oh, good. I thought maybe I had a wrong number. Anyway, I need to schedule a follow-up visit. I had my stress test a week ago."

Zarah's hands fumbled across the keyboard as she opened the scheduling software. "Okay…sir…what is…." She looked over the form on the screen. The first blank was for NAME. "Your…name?"

"Jerod Hunter."

She filled in the boxes. Next: DOB.

"Mr…" she looked back up at the name line, "…Hunter. I need your…date of birth."

"Twelve seventeen fifty-nine."

"What is your…phone number?"

He gave her the number.

"Thank you, Mr…" she looked back up at the NAME line, "Hunter." Next: DATE.

"And what…is the…date?"

"You don't know the date?"

Marathon's ass. She was failing. Like she knew she would. "I mean, the date you want the appointment. I think."

He gave her the date, and she scheduled him in the system.

"I have to say," he said, "this is the strangest phone call I've ever had at a doctor's office."

"I…usually file…papers and…bake cakes with my hamster."

"That's pretty depressing. Good luck."

"Thanks, sir." Zarah pressed "End Call."

The buttons blinked wildly.

"Write a script," Angie said over her shoulder. "It helps."

Zarah nodded, pulled off a blank memo sheet, and scripted, "Lark Springs Cardiology, this is Zarah. Can you hold, please?" Then she picked up the phone and pressed one of the blinking buttons.

At exactly 10:28, Zarah felt a stare boring into the back of her head.

"You too, Ms. Park," she said before she hung up the phone. Seeing that all other calls were being handled or on hold, she turned around.

Greg grinned and scratched the back of his neck.

Blood rushed to her cheeks as a smile spread across her face. "What—what are you doing here?"

Franklin waved from behind him. "Cancellation for 10:30. I called him myself. Come on back with us and help with his test."

Zarah looked at the blinking phone lines. Phones. Greg. Callers. Schedules. Appointments. Greg. "I…"

Franklin held a hand to his chest. "Are you, Zarah Smith, considering *not* abandoning your task to answer the calls of strangers?"

Maybe? Am I?

Franklin pretended to wipe tears from his eyes. "My little weirdo, my protégé, all grown up. But seriously," he said, composing himself, "Angie, can you and Brock cover for Zarah? Just for this test?"

"Sure, give me ten minutes," said Angie.

With all her calls forwarded to Angie and Brock, Zarah lifted herself from Lina's chair and started down the hallway toward Greg's exam room, where Franklin had probably already started the test. She let out an audible sigh, slackening her shoulders a bit, letting herself relish in her own silence. Soon she'd be in the safe zone, joking with Franklin, talking comics with Greg. Greg was finally getting his test, and soon he'd be able to get treatment.

I have a safe zone in a public place.

I can answer phones and talk to strangers.

And then she realized with a start: *I don't even need Z.*

Franklin burst into the hallway, phone pressed against his face. Zarah opened her mouth to speak, but Franklin's wide-eyed stare banished the sound.

He grabbed her arm with his free hand. "Start CPR. Now."

She blinked for a moment before he pushed her into the exam room.

Greg lay on the floor, lifeless.

But it couldn't be. She'd just talked to him fifteen minutes ago.

"3883 Olympic Way, Suite 205. Exam room 2," Franklin rattled off.

She looked at the still-running treadmill with electrodes dangling, rocking back and forth unsteadily. How long had he been on the treadmill before tachycardia? Did Franklin lay him down on the floor before he...?

"Unresponsive. Zarah—CPR—now."

And then she remembered this was Greg and his heart wasn't beating. She dropped to her knees next to him and stared at his bare chest. Was it chest compressions or breathing first? Chest compressions? Breathing? *Damnit, this is Greg!* She closed her eyes. *Remember!*

"Twenty-six. Male. Zarah—please!"

"Please!" Iris's voice sounded like it was tearing her

vocal chords. "Oh God! He's killing us!" She pounded on the door.

Zarah's eyes shot open. She was on the floor of the Babylonian storage closet, curled into fetal position.

Tearing scream.

Crack of the shotgun.

Thud against the closet door.

Click of the phone into the receiver.

"Jesus, Zarah! Use the AED! The kid's gonna fucking die!"

Whir of the treadmill.

Sterile voice of the AED.

Men and women bursting through the door.

Being carried, shoved.

And then she saw them.

A man and his two kids.

An elderly couple.

Iris.

Their blood looked just like it did in the movies. Pools, splatters, handprints. Thick like syrup. And red, the reddest red. It smelled.

Iris's eyes stared into nothing.

The paramedics knelt over Greg.

But he hadn't been shot.

He hadn't been there.

The paramedics backed away.

"Clear!"

His body jumped.

Where was she?

"Clear!"

His body jumped again.

A hand was on her shoulder. A man knelt in front of her. He looked like Franklin.

"He's breathing," he told her as she fell into his chest. "It's okay. He's breathing."

CHAPTER 19

Z was underground. Suffocating. Couldn't breathe. Remembering the Other children whispering, "Let the darkness touch it," as they'd buried her moments before.

Each time her chest expanded with breath, the vines cut deeper into her body, dust filled her lungs. She would cough, breathe in more dust, heave so that the vines tore and mangled her skin.

If she could just stop breathing.

If she could just die.

"Call someone," Franklin said.

Zarah was in his Hummer but she couldn't move.

Was she dead?

"Here," he said, tossing her a phone. It plopped into her lap. She reached for it, but her arm remained useless like a sack of sand.

"I took it from his bag," said Franklin. "We should call his friends and family before we get to the hospital."

Call whose friends and family? The Others are all dead.

"What the—what the hell are you muttering about, Zarah? I need you to call someone."

"I know, this is really Saint Anthony's job," Iris had said as she stood in the closet doorway. "But Saint Christopher always helps me. Here, keep him with you into the closet this time. He'll help you find

something for your thesis." As she pulled the chain from around her neck, her long, straight black hair shimmered.

Iris placed the medal around Zarah's neck, and her hazel eyes glittered with excitement. "Kalí tíhi. Good luck!" She smiled as she stepped out toward the exhibits and closed the closet door behind her.

Everyone's dead now. I'm dead, too. Z didn't live. Z didn't save anyone.

"Jesus. Okay, maybe I'm going at this all wrong."

The seat belt tightened across her torso and lap as her body lurched to the side like a doll's.

She blinked at the Hummer's gray interior. Its hazard lights click-clicked. Franklin grasped her shoulders firmly with both hands and pulled her toward him. She met his eyes, which were worn and sad like he'd been trying to cry but just didn't have the energy left.

Was this her funeral?

"It's me," he said. "Franklin. Greg had a heart attack 30 minutes ago. You know—135-pound comic book nerd with glasses. I need you to call someone, anyone on his phone. He needs his friends and family and you. Can you do that for me when I pull back onto the road?"

Her neck loosened. She turned her head to look out the window and realized they were pulled over in a restaurant's loading zone about four blocks from the hospital.

"Yes," she whispered.

"Good," said Franklin as he released Zarah and pulled back onto Main Street.

Call someone.

She looked at Greg's phone in her lap and tried to reach for it.

He'd had a heart attack.

He needed her.

He needed her to call.

She strained and stretched but her body refused. Tears welled in her eyes. She was nothing. She did nothing.

"You can do this, Zarah," said Franklin. "I saw you earlier, talking on the phone with strangers, scheduling appointments. You can do this."

She straightened her posture. He was right. She wasn't nothing: she was Zarah. She could talk to strangers on the phone. She could sing to her hamster.

She reached for the phone again. The sand flowed out of her arm, and she lifted Greg's phone from her lap. She ran her fingers over the cool screen.

What if she couldn't use the phone? What if she couldn't find his friends or his parents, or could find them but simply couldn't speak?

Zarah clutched at Iris's Saint Christopher medal with one hand as she grasped the phone with the other.

Zarah didn't believe in God, and she didn't believe in saints. She didn't even believe in Z, not really. But someone had to call, and she knew now that she could do it. She fiddled with the touch screen menus until she found Greg's recent calls. Zarah, Zarah, Comics Inked, Bastian. Yes, she remembered the name. That was definitely one of his roommates.

What now?

She held her breath and pressed "call."

"Greggie," answered a warm masculine voice after two rings. "Your tests are done early. How'd they go?"

This was it. This was Greg's real, live roommate. But what could she say? How could she tell him?

"Greggie? You there?"

"Lark Springs Cardiology," she recited from the script she'd memorized. What in Marathon's name was she doing? "This is Zarah. How may I direct your call?"

"Zarah? The Zarah? You do exist!"

"How may I help you?"

"And you're as quirky as Greggie made you out to be. How is he? How'd the tests go?"

Zarah opened her mouth but was silenced by the mental image of Greg's body jumping off the floor.

"Why are you calling from Greg's phone?" His voice hardened. "What's going on? Where's Greg?"

Greg had died.

"Zarah," Bastian's voice cracked. "Say something. Please."

"Please!" Iris's voice sounded like it was tearing her vocal chords. "Oh God! He's killing us!"

Zarah tried to reach the door handle. She strained and stretched and grasped but her body refused. Iris was screaming. Crying. And then—

Franklin pulled the phone out of Zarah's hand. "Mr. Normand is on his way to the hospital," he said. "My name is Franklin. I'm a nurse. I was getting him ready for testing when he had a heart attack." He paused. "I probably shouldn't have told you that. Damned HIPPA laws. I bet you're not on his emergency contact list." He paused again. "Twenty minutes? Good. I'll be the fat one in scrubs next to the redhead. And, hey, he'll be okay."

In the waiting room, Zarah sat down in a hard plastic chair, pulled her knees to her chest, and hugged Greg's messenger bag stuffed with his belongings. The hospital smelled like antiseptic, latex, and iodine. Like a dead band-aid. She peered around the room at the crying babies, makeshift bandages, and huddled families. One black-haired white woman sat alone across the room, praying the rosary.

"It might be a while before you get to see him," Franklin said as he sat down beside Zarah.

She watched the woman whispering to herself, face obscured by her bangs.

"Dr. Desai knows we're here, so as soon as she sees Greg, we'll know something."

Did she look like Iris just because Zarah was thinking about her?

"Are you okay?" asked Franklin.

"Are you injured?" asked the paramedic. She shook her head. A female officer handed her a bottle of water. A male officer put his arm around her, guided her between the pools of blood, Iris's blood, over

the splatters, like mud puddles. "There's no longer an active shooter," the male officer said. "Officer Cortez will debrief you across the street."

"Earth to Planet Zarah. Are you there?"

She watched as the woman looked up. Much younger than Iris. Paler. Softer features.

"Sorry." Zarah turned to Franklin. "I'll be fine."

"You look the damned opposite of fine. You're whispering some scary shit to yourself."

"It's...nothing. How long until we hear from Dr. Desai?"

Franklin rested a hand on her shoulder. "You know, Zarah, it's not 'nothing' to watch someone be—"

"How long until we hear from Dr. Desai?" she repeated.

He rubbed his hands over his face. "I honestly don't know. Could be hours. But hey," he added, punching her shoulder and feigning a smile, "how about we get some lunch from the cafeteria after his friends get here? Because I know how you get when you're not fed regularly."

Zarah looked away and noticed the woman with the black hair wasn't actually praying a rosary. She was playing on her phone.

Iris and not Iris. Praying and not praying.

Zarah thought of the Chordinator, the way he had been Behnam and not Behnam, and maybe not even there at all. What else was she mis-seeing? She'd seen Greg last night and had known to call 9-1-1, but she hadn't called. Had she simply convinced herself that the symptoms had gone away when they really hadn't? Was she the reason he'd had a heart attack? Died? Because he *had died.*

"Start CPR. Now."

Tried to reach. Strained and stretched and grasped but her body refused.

"Parakalo, Zarah, let me in!"

"Jesus Zarah! Use the AED!"

"Please! Oh god!"

"The kid's gonna fucking die!"

"He's still fuckin' alive, right?"

She didn't know that voice.

Zarah looked up. A tall, unkempt blond white man in his upper 20s lumbered toward them in torn jeans and a beer-stained white undershirt, followed by an brown-skinned man of similar age with a chiseled jaw and turquoise tie. They didn't have crying babies or bandages or rosaries.

What were they doing here?

The man in the tie met Zarah's eyes and grinned. "Calm down, Fred," he said with a warm voice that she recognized from the phone as Bastian's. "We've found her." He stopped just in front of her and held out his hand. "Zarah. What a terrible way to meet you, but I guess we don't get to pick these things."

Zarah stared at his hand. She knew she was supposed to take it. But even her brain felt filled with sand.

"Greggie hasn't stopped talking about you for the past two weeks."

She looked back up at his face, his smile, his lightly age-creased eyes. She had never, ever met this man before, but something about him, be it the warmth of his voice or the sheer absence of insidiousness in his smile, had enough Greg in it that she knew the two men had formed an impression on one another. Shaking hands with him was shaking hands with a piece of Greg.

The sand drained from her body, and she stood and took his hand. "Zarah."

"And this is—"

"I can introduce myself. Damn." The blond man straightened his posture and adjusted a collar that wasn't there. "I'm Fred."

He was shifting his weight, rubbing bloodshot eyes, fidgeting at his sides.

Graham crackers, he's more worried than I am.

Zarah offered her hand, and he pulled absently at his

pockets a moment before he shook it.

Franklin followed suit, shaking hands with each of them. "Franklin. I'm a nurse. I was with Greg when he had the heart attack."

"And it's all your fault, Justine!" shouted Fred.

Bastian patted Fred on the shoulder. "Please excuse this guy. He's operating off three hours of sleep and a lifetime of jackassery."

Franklin nodded. "I sympathize with his plight, particularly the latter. But it looks like Greg's going to be all right, and it's unlikely Justine's or anyone's fault. Follow me, and I'll catch you up in the cafeteria. Lunch is on me."

Lunch consisted of forks clinking against plates, Fred slurping his soup, and the obligatory game of, "So how do you know Greg?" Zarah almost wished Kris were there to lick the icing off a piece of cake, just for the distraction. Uneaten sandwich in front of her, she clutched Greg's messenger bag in her lap, running her fingers over the hard corners of what she assumed was his sketchbook inside the bag.

"We met in high school," Bastian said. "Partners in gym class."

Would it be wrong of her to take a look through the book? To page through something so much like a diary while the artist, the author, lay unconscious and helpless in a hospital bed?

"I had to fight Fred here because he was picking on Greg. Remember what I said about that lifetime of jackassery?"

How many drawings were inside? What did they look like? More of Purgatory USA, Jude's gold wings, Z?

She thought about his drawing of Z hanging in her apartment, the gentle shading, the light stippling of her freckles, even a couple across her lips. Why did he take the time to draw something so detailed for her?

She knew why. He'd told her. And she'd never said it

back.

"Text from Dr. Desai," said Franklin as he placed a piece of cake in front of her. She stared at it the same blank way she'd stared at the sandwich he'd brought her. "He's awake. They're only letting family see him, but I can sneak one of you back for a few minutes."

Zarah sat straight up and looked at Bastian and Fred, who both looked back at her.

"Oh, hell," said Fred, "Greg would damn sure rather see your face than either of ours."

"Would you like to go, Zarah?" Bastian asked.

Of course she wanted to see him, to throw her arms around him, to prove beyond a doubt that he was once again living and breathing, to tell him, "Greg, I think I might love you too." But he would be weak, and he would need her to be strong. Could she keep from falling to pieces?

She nodded.

"Good," said Bastian. "Tell him his parents' flight takes off in an hour. And that Fred and I love him."

"That's heavy, man," said Fred. "But yeah, I guess we do."

Franklin led Zarah through the hospital, up the elevator, down a corridor, and through a buzzer-locked door. Finally they reached Greg's room, and Franklin creaked the door open. "Go ahead," he said, motioning her in. "You don't need a chaperone."

Zarah tip-toed into the room, lit only through the blinds of a large window. Greg lay still and silent, eyes closed, connected to at least three beeping machines. He looked terribly tiny, like an actual stick figure beneath bleached white hospital blankets.

Greg stirred for a moment, squinted his eyes, then settled. "Zarah?"

"Yes."

"I thought you were another angel," he said. "My red-haired queen, prettiest face that I have ever seen," he whisper-sang. He patted the bed. "Come on, make yourself at home."

She stepped forward and perched on the edge of his bed.

His barely-open eyes appraised her without his glasses. He looked strange without them. A little divot remained on each side of the bridge of his nose, tiny craters. She felt his hand grasp hers.

"Did you get the license plates on the six trains that just ran me over?" He lifted his free hand and brought it about an inch from his eyes. "Zarah, is that a needle in my skin?"

She nodded.

"What—what happened to me?"

How could she tell him? How could she say it?

"I take your silence to mean it was bad."

He needed her to be strong. "Heart attack," she whispered.

He lowered his hand and pursed his lips. "Fantastic," he groaned. "Like, I thought it would just be the fainting, you know? Like I could just be normal, and not be the dying boy." He released her hand and began to fumble with his bed tray. He grabbed the pink plastic vomit pan, holding it an inch from his face.

"What do you need?"

"My phone." Greg held a box of tissues to his eyes. "I want to show you a song."

"Oh," Zarah said, digging through his bag to find his phone and ear buds. "Here. I was holding onto it for you."

He took his phone and ear buds as she handed them to him. "Bastian talked to your parents," she said as he scrolled through his phone. "Their plane is taking off in an hour."

"Bastian? My parents? I hope that doesn't mean Fred is here too?"

"He's here."

"Wow. This is going to be a three-ringed circus of

embarrassment. Can't a guy just have a heart attack in solitude? I mean, relative solitude, with just you?"

"Your friends seem nice."

"If Fred seems nice, something's wrong."

"Well..."

"Oh, yeah. Heart attack." He shook his head. "I want the story. But not now. Later, when I'm like actually completely awake. Because I think I'm probably really asleep right now. But here," he said, placing one ear bud in his ear and handing the other to her. "I'll show you that song."

She hesitated. Music took her places. And she really, really needed to just stay here.

"I know music isn't your thing, but please?"

He was so thin. His hair matted. His nose divoted. Maybe she wouldn't go anywhere in her head. Maybe she could be strong and stay right here. As she placed the ear bud in her ear, a gentle sound like water dropping onto liquid guitar strings plodded in Zarah's right ear. Slowly, drums faded in and built to a crescendo. She concentrated hard on the sound, on Greg's face, on not going places in her head.

Greg rested his phone on his stomach and let his hands fall to his sides. "Do you see it?" he whispered.

"See what?"

"Jude is holding Z. And she's crying." Greg's heavy eyes closed.

"Why is she crying?"

"Don't you see it? He loves her." He breathed deeply. "The music will show you," he whispered as he drifted back to sleep. She watched his chest rise and fall, rise and fall for the remainder of the song, just to be sure. Then she stood, pulled the ear bud from her ear, and nestled it into his. Quietly, she sifted through a plastic bag on his bed tray, where she found his glasses, unfolded them, and placed them on his face. She fluffed his matted hair and kissed his forehead. "I'm starting to love you, too," she whispered before leaving him to his music and his dreams.

"Yes, yes, he's fine. He's awake," said Bastian into his phone as Zarah and Franklin approached him and Fred in the waiting room. "Here's Zarah now! How was he?"

"Tired," she said. "Fell back asleep listening to music."

"Did you hear that? Yeah, I know, Greggie and his music. Can't wait to see you either. Bye." He put the phone in his pocket. "So what did he say?" he asked Zarah. "How did he seem? Was he lucid? In good spirits?"

Zarah laughed. "He said you, Fred, and his parents would be a 'three-ringed circus of embarrassment.'"

"Well, thank God he's himself. Franklin, what's the chance of him receiving more visitors?"

"Nil," said Franklin. "At least for now, I'd say go home and take a nap. I'll text you if things change."

"What about Zarah?" asked Fred.

"She's coming with us," said Bastian. "We'll play Rock On: Eighties Edition. Maybe Zarah can beat Greg's high score on 'The Final Countdown.'"

A boyish grin spread across Fred's face.

Zarah held Greg's messenger bag tight against her chest like armor and started to shake her head. Go to Greg's apartment with his stranger-roommates and play pretend guitar when she hadn't taken out her real one in two years? She'd rather elope with the Chordinator.

"The Fiiii-nal Count-dowwwwwn!" the boys sang in unison.

The song flooded her memory with Greg flying her cutout of stick-figure-Z around her apartment, swooping and tilting. Her heart swelled at the thought of him, at the thought of holding a stupid plastic guitar and pressing buttons to beat his score on his favorite song. Something to surprise him with, to goad him to get better and come home. She sighed. "I'll go."

"Behold, the power of Greggie!" shouted Bastian as he high-fived Fred.

Franklin tousled her hair. "Take care of yourself."

CHAPTER 20

"I used to play guitar," Zarah said as she buckled herself into the front leather seat of Bastian's Acura TSX. "So maybe I'll have an edge on Greg's high score. But I haven't played in two years." She paused. "I'm not sure why I'm telling you this."

"Because you're so damned emotionally tired that your brain broke?" offered Fred from the back seat.

Zarah shrugged. "That sounds accurate."

"Trust me," said Fred, "I'm familiar with the feeling."

Bastian started the car, and the twang of country music blasted through the speakers. He turned it down a notch. "Sorry," he said as he pulled out of the parking spot. "We thought if we played the music loud enough on the way here, we wouldn't have to think."

"Are you all three from Texas, then?" asked Zarah, gesturing to the speakers.

"Damn straight," said Fred, leaning up between the seats. He smelled like old cigarettes and tequila. "Greg was ready to get the hell outta there."

"I don't think any of us favored Wilford much by the time we left."

"Wilford was fine. Just that…one individual needed to

go. I won't call her what I was going to in the presence of a lady."

Bastian laughed. "You do need a nap, Fred. You're starting to sound like half a gentleman."

A few minutes later, they parked the car—mercifully close since the sidewalks were flooded with lunchtime walkers—and approached an old brick building. Bastian opened the door, and Zarah's eyes widened at an intricate wooden staircase inside, its red carpet, and wings on each side of its landing. The wood was dusty and the carpet was stained and threadbare, but it looked like it could have been the staircase from *Gone With the Wind* years ago. It was far nicer than her rusting metal stairs, at least.

"I bet this used to be beautiful," she said as they climbed the staircase. She imagined Scarlett O'Hara standing at the top. *Wait. Scarlett. Baby Scarlett.* Lina had had her baby! She should call Lina, text her, see how they were doing.

"Just wait 'til you see our apartment," said Fred. "It looks like an old asylum room. This is just what they showed to the fancy visitors."

But his voice seemed far away, background noise, as Zarah thought about Lina. How could she have had lunch with Lina at least once a week and then become so closed-off after the internship that she didn't even notice her friend was pregnant?

"First of all, Fred," said Bastian, "there aren't any 'fancy visitors' to mental institutions. Second of all, this was a music conservatory."

She wondered why Lina had continued for months to ask Zarah to lunch, only to be met with a sullen, silent shake of Zarah's head, until one day Lina just gave up and stopped asking.

"Likely cover," said Fred. "Mad musical geniuses sent off to a 'conservatory' when they were really experimented on. The same way Justine treated my heart."

Graham crackers, Zarah thought, *even if I did try to text Lina, I don't have a damned phone.*

The whole thing seemed silly as she reached the landing and followed Fred and Bastian down the hall of the right wing. Who might have tried to call between the time she shut down her phone and the time the contract ran out? Who might have texted? Were there messages floating around somewhere in cyberspace? From Lina? From her roommates? From Behn?

No, Behnam would have called her dad.

But still.

"Here it is," said Fred, flourishing his hand in front of a door that matched the red of the carpet. "The asylum torture room."

Bastian shook his head as he unlocked and opened the door. "Please stop."

"No," said Fred as they walked inside. "I will never stop believing in this conspiracy."

Inside, office-style pock-marked carpeting, a water-stained ceiling, and cracked white walls enclosed a living room nearly the same size as Zarah's entire apartment. An over-sized TV was perched on a small entertainment center, accented by a plywood table propped on tires in front of a hideous lime green couch. Everything smelled like stale cheese curls.

"Why do you still have Greg's bag?" asked Fred.

Zarah looked down at her chest, where she was still hugging Greg's bag like a life preserver. She'd forgotten she'd had it. Why hadn't she left it with him in the hospital?

"Oh, leave her alone, Fred," said Bastian. "We're all a little shook up."

"I didn't mean anything by it. Jesus." Fred paused. "Greg said you wouldn't ever come to visit us because we smell."

"Fred, it's you. You're the one who smells." Bastian sighed. "So, Zarah. Have you ever played *Rock On: Eighties*

Edition?"

She shook her head.

"Well, you're in for a treat. Or a dose of unnecessary carpal tunnel syndrome from a fake guitar." He turned on the TV and gaming console, then reached behind the entertainment center to pull out two plastic guitars. Zarah had seen the game before at Boulder. Students would press buttons on fake guitars and pretend they were playing music. She and Behnam would roll their eyes at each other, wondering why no one ever took them up on their offers to teach them to play an actual guitar. But—she thought as Bastian handed her a plastic guitar covered in colorful buttons—if it meant a lot to Greg and his friends, she'd give it a try.

"Rock, paper, scissors?" Fred asked Bastian.

"Nah," Bastian said as he handed the second guitar to Fred, "you'd better play before you pass out.

The game started with a loud G chord, and flames shaped the words "Get ready to ROCK!" across both sides of a split screen. As the words melted, guitar strings and frets with red, orange, yellow, white, and blue dots bled into view. Zarah put the guitar strap around her back and adjusted the plastic instrument in her hands, nestling it next to Greg's messenger bag. It was smaller than a real guitar, thinner, lighter. The synthesizer intro began, and Zarah followed the dots on the screen as they lit in-time with the music, hitting each corresponding button with her fingers in time with the ten-measure opening riff. Five thumbs-up spread across her screen.

Piece of high-altitude cake. She smiled despite herself, thinking of Greg flying stick-figure Z around her apartment and singing, "Dee-dee-dum—dum—dee-dee-dum-dah-dummmm!"

The drums broke in, building on the simple riff. She plugged along, perfect score, catching a glimpse of Fred, whose tongue was out in concentration. Joey Tempest's voice sang from the speakers. The notes were still easy, simple, repetitive. She imagined herself leaning against the dorm wall, making up an acoustic version. She could almost feel the bite of the strings under the tips of her fingers, feel the weight of her Fender's hips.

"It's the fiii-nal couuuunt-doooowwwn!" Fred and Bastian sang along with Joey Tempest. They both grinned at her expectantly.

"Get ready," said Fred. "This solo is gonna kick both our asses."

"For Greggie!" Bastian cheered.

"For Greggie," Zarah said with a nod and a smile. She narrowed her eyes to join the boys as they sang, "The fiii-nal couuuunt-doooowwwn!"

Then a cluster of blue, orange, white, red, and yellow appeared on the screen, and rapid guitar notes, like rippling water, blasted from the TV. *Graham crackers.* She'd forgotten about hair metal's absurd solos. She stalked each colorful dot with her eyes, fingers sweating and sliding across the buttons, pressing a few wrong ones at the wrong times. But five thumbs-up still remained across the top of her screen.

As the knot of colors dissipated and the synthesizer riff began again, Zarah knew she was on the home stretch.

"Holy shit, dude."

"No fucking way, man."

"It's not even real," she said over the riff.

"But you're better than Greggie!" said Bastian.

She imagined him home from the hospital, jumping up and down on the couch and zooming paper superheroes around, singing along with his friends.

"It's the fiii-nal couuuunt-doooowwwn!" the boys continued to sing.

On the last note, Zarah gently pressed the strum button.

"WINNER!" blazed across her screen, followed by, "New High Score." She entered her name: "Z."

Fred reached out and shook Zarah's hand. "Zarah, I

hope you fucking marry Greg. That was badass."

"Well as much as I'd like my own chance at getting slaughtered," said Bastian, "I think I'm going to change into pajamas, email my boss, and pass out. Fred, I demand that you bathe and sleep. And Zarah, you may do whatever the hell you want, but I'll show you Greg's room just in case you want to take a nap there. Because apparently, tragedy makes us all toddlers."

Zarah nodded and went to put the plastic guitar behind the entertainment center.

"Oh, leave it on the couch," he said with a grin, "I'll need to defend Fred's honor later." He motioned for her to follow him.

Zarah walked behind him past the TV and down a blank-walled hallway to Greg's room, the first door on the left. Inside, the walls of Greg's room were adorned with exactly three band posters, none of which she recognized. For furniture, he had a bed covered with a gray comforter; a peeling black computer desk; five sideways-stacked crates full of crisply-folded tee-shirts, jeans, and flannel; and a seven-foot-tall bookshelf bursting with sleeved comics.

It was strange to see his room for the first time without him there, as if she were in an exhibit of a not-so-historical home, with everything staged just as the owner might have had it. *Mr. Normand made his bed each morning,* she imagined the curator saying. *These band posters are originals that belonged to Mr. Normand himself. We cannot guess as to whether these were favorites or just wall-fillers, as Mr. Normand's digital collections have been lost over the years, but—*

"Hey," said Bastian.

She turned to face him.

"Look, I know you can be really shy, and Fred and I are probably a lot to take, especially after, well, you know, the hospital and all." He looked down at his polished shoes to collect his thoughts. "But Greggie likes you. A lot. And I can already see how much you care about him. I just want you to know that if you're going to be sticking around in Greggie's life—and I seriously hope you are—I want you to feel like you can trust us." He paused and looked at her, appraising her, as if he saw something that made him deeply sad for just a fraction of a second. Then he grinned again. "Stay here as long as you want. I'll even try to get Fred to bathe once a day." He chuckled at his own joke.

"Thanks," whispered Zarah, and he waved as he shut the door on his way out.

She blinked at the door. *Graham crackers, what was that?* Had Greg told him to say all that? No, he couldn't have. She hadn't planned to be here. She would never normally be here, alone in her sort-of-boyfriend's apartment, playing video games—a guitar video game—with his roommates. Everything was changing so quickly, moving around her while she stood still. She wouldn't normally trust these strange men, even if they were Greg's friends. She wouldn't even normally trust Greg. But Greg was—well, *Greg*—and he was sick and his friends were sad, and nothing had been normal since she met him.

She glanced around Greg's room again, trying to put her thoughts aside, at the posters, the clothes, and of course his comic collection. "Let's see what Mr. I Hate the Indomitable X thinks is brilliant literature," she muttered as she stepped toward the bookshelf.

There were, of course, the obligatory Marvel and DC Comics, a complete or nearly-complete collection of *Harbinger*, then some graphic novels—*Fun Home* and *The Sandman*. But as she scanned through, one odd-ball caught her eye: his signed copy of *Kris the Sad Rhinoceros*.

A tiny purple rhinoceros frowned at her from the spine of the book. In all the chaos of the day, she'd forgotten Kris or Morrow or whoever had written this book. Zarah pulled it off the shelf and examined the thick-lined, cartoony style of the front cover. She pondered opening it, wondering what kind of story lay inside. One about a cranky office manager who hated everyone, "The End"?

She shook her head and placed it back on the shelf. Maybe another time. For now, she wanted to explore more of this Greg exhibit—not to pry, of course—but just to look at what was on open display. As she ran her fingers along the spines of his comics, she hoped she'd find just one secret issue of *The Indomitable X*. One issue to show he'd considered the trend for a moment. *After all*, she thought as she futilely reached the last shelf, *X is certainly less ridiculous than an angel fighting the Universe embodied.*

The Universe. Jude. She remembered she was wearing his messenger bag and that his sketchbook was inside, still unopened. It couldn't be wrong just to look. He'd let her see the drawings before. It wasn't the same as looking through a diary or tax returns or something.

She dug through his bag and pulled out the sketchbook.

She flipped past Purgatory USA and several iterations of Jude, each just as lovingly detailed as the last. *Greg has to get better*, she thought as she traced her fingers across Jude's wings. *This talent, this gift—he should actually illustrate a comic. What if we told a story together? What if we told the story of Jude and Z? I already know he can draw her—*

The bursting cleavage of what could only be described as porn star Z interrupted her thoughts. Gone were her carefully-shaded ringlets, her lightly-stippled freckles, the hint of pain behind her dark, masked eyes. In their place were thick, voluptuous waves, airbrushed foundation, and fake eyelashes. Her dress was merely a strip of fabric wrapped in a Z shape across her body.

Zarah wanted to throw her a robe, give her a bath. What the fuck was this?

Well, she *knew* what it was. She looked at the way the fabric strip clung to Z's buttocks and realized Greg wasn't imagining Z. He was imagining *her*. Her cheeks flushed red. She wouldn't look like that in a strip of fabric. She'd have poofy hair, no cleavage, no hips, no muscles of any kind. What was he expecting?

And what the hell gave him the gall to draw this anyway?

She should close the book. She wasn't meant to see this. It was definitely like looking through his diary. But then she noticed deep red shading peeking through on the page underneath.

She shouldn't look. She definitely shouldn't look.

She turned the page.

Her blood rushed in her ear drums. Her heart pounded in her head. The bottom dropped out of her stomach like on a roller coaster.

It was her.

Not Z, but her. Zarah.

Zarah with the police officer outside the museum, but he was Jude.

"Please!" Iris's voice sounded like it was tearing her vocal chords. "Oh God! He's killing us!"

She ran her fingers over Z's curls, over Jude's outspread gold wings.

"There's no longer an active shooter." The officer's voice was calm, matter-of-fact. "Officer Cortez will debrief you across the street."

Blue and purple and green blotches began to cloud her sight. Her heart beat faster. Jude and Zarah and the whole page began to fade away.

She looked into the officer's watery eyes. He was broken, she could tell. He wanted to cry. The families, the children, the blood, the smell. You're not supposed to see a thing like that, even if you are a cop. You're not supposed to see it. She shouldn't have seen it. Couldn't have. It can't have happened. She stretched her arms as far as she could around the officer's torso as her knees buckled and her face contorted into a sob.

"I didn't let her in," she cried into his stomach. "I'll go back. I'll let her in. Please, please let me go back. Let me let her in. I swear. I'll do it. I swear. Please just let me go back."

Her vision was nearly black now.

The drawing was just like her and the officer. *Greg knows.* He must have seen the picture in the news two years ago.

How long had he known? Had he hidden it from her?

How could he understand her? How could he love her, if he knew they were all dead because of her? Dead like the Others, whom Z had immolated in her escape from her grave. Dead like he would be, had it been left to her shaking in a corner.

She needed to be home. Home with X. But she couldn't move. Couldn't reach. Couldn't—

She heard the music in her head, and it was deafening. It was Behnam. It was the Chordinator. It was the Others. She was in the catacombs, not ripe for excavation and discovery, but haunted with ghosts.

"No," Zarah whispered, trying to pull herself back to the present. But the ghosts from the catacombs pulled her into their tombs, suffocating her.

They were all there. Iris, everyone. All fourteen.

She shut her eyes and lowered herself to the floor as they closed in on her, as she let them bury her like the Others had buried Z.

CHAPTER 21

The guitar-and-drum mini symphonies of Explosions in the Sky continued to play through Greg's ear buds, shaping Jude and Z out of the ethereal pencils and ink of his dreams. He started with their interwoven hands in the center of his mind, then sketched their bodies, the Earth below their feet, and the Universe surrounding them.

Jude spread his gold wings, glistening in the pure starlight of outer space. The brilliant red of Z's hair popped of the page of Greg's dreaming mind. They gently lifted off from Earth like balloons and flew to the moon for bouncing, Venus for mimosas in the sunrise, and Jupiter for espresso at the Red Spot Cafe. They shot out to an ice bar on Neptune, sporting fur-lined hoods, and swung their feet as they sat on the edge of Saturn's rings on the way back to Earth.

"I think I love you," Jude whispered in Z's ear as they gazed at the moons and moonlets floating around them on Saturn. She didn't respond. He looked over at her, and she was grinning, and she was Zarah now with all her freckles and halo of hair. Then was Greg, and she kissed him hard as she reached her hands under his shirt and onto his stomach, all the while thrusting her tongue into his mouth. She ran her palms over his chest and to his shoulders, where she dug in her nails and pulled him down on top of her. His heart thudded against his chest and he kissed her back, wanting to share his

warmth with hers, longing to be inside her.

She unzipped his pants. He reached for her shorts, but they were no longer there. She was still Zarah, but now she was wearing Z's costume strapped tight across her body. Her nipples pushed hard through the fabric, her abs formed gentle slopes pointing down to where her mini-skirt was up and open, and she leaned in close and whispered, "Yes," in his ear, easing herself—

"Most holy apostle, Saint Jude," boomed his father's voice. "Faithful servant and friend of Jesus!"

The pulse in his groin collided to a halt. Heat dissipated to the chill of the air-conditioned church of his childhood, and Zarah's supple body underneath him turned to the cotton of his own pressed collared shirt and khakis. He sat up. At the front of the church stood his dad, wearing the green vestments of Ordinary Time. Explosions in the Sky continued to build and fade over the church speakers.

His dad adjusted his bifocals on a younger, line-less face from Greg's childhood, hair still a dark brown instead of gray. As usual, he didn't stand at the pulpit, but walked freely around the church.

"The Church honors and invokes you universally as the patron of hope. Please intercede on Greg's behalf." He gestured to Greg and looked toward the heavens.

They're praying for me? *Greg looked around the church, filled with abstract, faceless silhouettes.* Damn, maybe I am a hopeless case. I was just getting laid on Saturn, and now I'm…here. In church. With my dad. And shadow people.

Then his mother was beside him, young, too, like his father. Her hair was shoulder-length and ironed straight the way it used to be when he was a boy. She rested a hand on Greg's shoulder and prayed softly, "Saint Jude, come to our son's assistance in this great need as he recovers from…" Her lip quivered and her eyebrows softened, which Greg knew betrayed a sadness she was trying to hide.

"Naomi," said Greg's father, "it's okay to cry. Yes, God brought him back to us, but we can still grieve."

The church faded into darkness. Greg's eyelids felt at once heavy and spring-loaded.

"Aloysius, look! He hears us praying."

As Greg blinked his eyes open, he heard a persistent beeping over his music, felt a pinch on top of his left hand, smelled the heavy antiseptic only used in the deepest recesses of intensive care. Encompassing his field of vision were the lined, properly-aged faces of his parents.

"Oh, my Greggie!" cracked the voice of his mother, who now allowed tears to flow freely. She gripped his right hand.

Greg sighed. "Well, I must be actually awake. No part of my psyche can so accurately portray this level of melodrama."

She cried harder.

"Oh, mom, I'm only joking." He squeezed her hand.

"Do you know why you're here, Greg?" his father asked with genuine interest.

Greg looked at his parents' bloodshot eyes, at his IV, at the electrodes stuck to his chest underneath his flimsy hospital gown. He touched his ear buds, still playing music, and remembered the angel, remembered Zarah, gently handing them to him.

Heart attack, she'd told him. *A fucking heart attack. No wonder they're a mess.*

He removed his ear buds and nodded.

In the absence of music, thoughts pummeled his mind. *How much is this going to cost? What about the ambulance? What about work? I can't take time off. Val's going to have to replace me and then I'll have no job and I'll have to leave Colorado and move back in with my parents where public health care is a joke and I'll be unemployed and dying and do I need surgery? How in the fuck will I pay for surgery? And what day is it? When did this happen? How long have I been sleeping? And where was I when—? In the doctor's office, I think. The last thing I remember is talking to Zarah and...*

Zarah. She was here, or at least I think she was. But if I went code blue in the doctor's office, does that mean...did she see it? Oh God, I hope not. He thought about her telling him the story of Z's moment of greatness, the way all the life in her seemed to die during that story. *She's already seen more shit in her life than anyone needs to.*

I've got to find her. He reached for his phone but immediately remembered he couldn't text her landline. Could he avoid calling her in front of his parents? Maybe she was still at the hospital.

"Have you seen Fred or Bastian yet?" he asked his parents.

"Sebastian!" said his mother with a smile. "No, are they here?"

"They were, but—"

"Greg," started his father, "we really need to talk about what happened. We need to decide how to move forward with your treatment options."

"I know, and we will," he said as he texted Bastian. "But right now, I need something."

Greg: Is Zarah with you?

Bastian: Yes. Asleep in your room for the past hour.

"We can get whatever you need," said his mother. "We even picked you up a comic book in the gift shop to keep you from getting bored."

Greg: Is she okay?

Bastian: None of us are. Can we come visit?

"Greggie, are you listening to me?"

He looked up from his phone. His mom was holding out a fresh comic book, and before his hand touched the newsprint, he recognized the garish colors, the crispness of a high-budget comic. Rob Eager's mainstream ilk. But his mother was grinning the way she had when she'd saved up to buy him designer cowboy boots in fourth grade and he'd hated the mere thought of them, but he'd worn them and acted damned happy about it because that was the right thing to do.

"Thanks, Mom," he said through a forced smile, mustering all the energy he could. He took the comic and examined the cover. It was last month's issue, the cover featuring TIX pressing a foot on Dr. Nemesinister's ridiculous throat.

"They didn't have a sketchbook," said his father, "but they did have some spare crayons and construction paper in the children's ward."

"You took art supplies from sick kids?" shouted Greg as he sat upright, just before a wave of exhaustion forced him back against his pillows.

"We did no such thing," said his mother. "They offered them freely."

TIX and stolen sick children's art supplies. Throw in a hospital clown making balloon animals out of condoms, and this day has the makings of a brilliant tragicomedy of errors. "Thank you both," he said. "These will tide me over until Bastian can bring my stuff from home."

Greg: Bring my sketchbook and a stack of my comics. Otherwise I will die here.

"Can Bastian bring some coffee?" asked his dad. "Turkish coffee."

"Dad, are you serious?"

"And whiskey," chimed in his mom. "Irish."

"Good lord, you two."

Greg: Also coffee and whiskey and pretend they're Turkish and Irish.

Bastian: Got it. Is your sketchbook in your bag?

Greg: Maybe?

**Bastian: I'll ask Zarah when she wakes up.
She's been carrying it around all day.**

"Shit," he said aloud.

"What, what's wrong?" asked his mother.

She's got my bag, which means she's got my sketchbook, which means she's got that pornographic picture of her as a superhero. What if it freaks her out? Or worse, what if it doesn't, and she actually wants to have sex with me, but here I am in the hospital with a defective heart and I don't even know if I can have *sex without* dying *on top of her.*

"Are you in pain?" asked his father.

Yes. Pain. Lots of it. In my battered soul.

Then he remembered the other drawing, the one of Jude holding Zarah. The one modeled after the picture in the newspaper.

"Do you want us to call a nurse?" his father persisted.

She doesn't know that I know what happened to her.

"Fuck." *I don't even know if* she *knows what happened to her. What if she remembers? What if she can't handle that? What if—*

Greg's father took his hand. "What's going on, son?"

Greg looked at his dad's lined face and remembered Bastian's advice to talk to them. It was true, his parents had always been supportive of Greg's decision not to go to college, of Joan's decision to use her MFA as a tattoo artist, of Bastian when he came out to them before he came out to his own parents. They'd supported Greg's choice to move to Colorado on a whim. They could be lecturey, and they were *so very* Catholic, but their lectures were often wise and always, always focused on love. He knew they'd love Zarah like their own and would support both of them now.

"Dad, Mom, when do you finally feel like an adult? Like a real one who can handle adult problems?"

They both considered the question for a moment, his

dad humming softly.

"When Jesus left his disciples," said his mom, cocking her head to the side like she always did when telling a story, "when they knew he would die, they were terrified to be left alone without his guidance. They didn't know who to turn to." She shrugged. "Jesus gave them chapters of advice, warnings of what life would be like for them, but nothing could really prepare them for that feeling of loss, of having to become the leader, the adult." She paused and patted Greg's hand. "It was like that when I left the convent. I didn't know what I was doing. I broke away from a sisterhood that I loved dearly but somehow still felt wrong in my heart. I've made a lot of mistakes, but I kept moving forward, and for me, that's what made me become an adult."

"I still don't feel like an adult, son," said his dad. "You never really know what you're doing. But being an adult means that you try because no one else can do it for you. You won't ever have all the answers, but you have to try whatever you can, and you have to learn from your wrong choices. Being an adult is living with uncertainty and still taking responsibility for it."

"Does any of that help?" asked his mom.

Greg sighed. "So what you're telling me is that being an adult is the worst feeling in the world."

"No, not always," she said. "There's freedom in it, and when you learn and then do something right the next time, there's a power, an exhilaration."

"But then there's always something new," added his dad.

"I'm not sure you guys are helping."

"If it's the medical bills that have you worried, we'll figure it out," said his dad. "And if it's your heart, we haven't talked about this yet, but it's very treatable."

Greg looked at his electrodes. "I'd actually momentarily forgotten about that. But thanks."

"What's going on, then?" asked his dad.

"I met someone."

"Oh?"

"And…there's something big. Something I know I need to grow up and deal with, but I don't know how. And I'm not sure she would want me to tell you about it yet."

His mother straightened her back.

"Son," his father said in his measured deacon's voice. "Every child is a blessing. It's difficult. Raising you and Joan was a joy, but there were many trials, and—"

"Wait—what? You think I got her *pregnant*?"

His father shrugged. "That's normally how this talk starts."

"No. No, no. Absolutely not. I literally just met her and our date was baking a cake."

His parents softened their postures.

Greg looked at his phone, wishing he could text Zarah, wishing he could check in on her, tell her how he felt. "I think I love her. I mean, well, I do. I do love her. She's going through some pretty big stuff and I want to help her. But then I went and *died* and came back to life and now I'm stuck here and I don't know if she can handle all this. She doesn't have a bunch of friends and family like I do. She just has a hamster."

"And you," said his mother.

"And what good am I?" Greg said, gesturing to himself. "I'm hooked up to machines. I'm useless."

"Greg, I know you're scared. But we talked with Dr. Desai and she thinks a standard surgery called ablation can help you. And she can get you on the schedule as early as this week."

"But how will I pay for that? My insurance isn't free."

"You are our son," said his mom. "God's precious gift. We'll make it work. The hospital offers payment plans. But for now, you should rest. That way you'll have energy when your friends get here."

"Bastian told me you'd give me good advice," said

Greg said with a smile as he closed his eyes.

CHAPTER 22

Crack!-Crack!-Crack!

Shotgun.

Her eyes burst open. She was in a strange room, on the floor. High-pitched, blood-curdling screams erupted outside the door. Indistinct shouting. Pounding feet. Shattering glass.

She lay still as if she were dead. She tried to breathe, but her lungs were paralyzed.

"Fuck yeah! Got him!" shouted a man's familiar voice.

"Parakalo, Zarah, let me in!" cried Iris in her head.

Crack!-Crack!-Crack!

Can't breathe.

"Another one! Hey Bastian, you gotta join next round."

"Shit, Fred. You can't play that while Zarah's here."

"Please!" Iris's voice tore at Zarah's mind. "Oh God! He's killing us!"

"Why not? I was gonna ask her to play when she gets up."

"Fred. Don't. Trust me. You gotta turn it off."

Crack!-Crack!-Crack!

"No!" Iris cried, her voice guttural, visceral. "He's coming! Zarah, he's coming!"

Crack!-Crack!-Crack!

"Pater hēmōn, ho en—"

Boom!

"That's how you fucking play!"

"Turn that shit off, Fred. Now."

"Okay, *Dad*. Christ."

Silence.

Air filled Zarah's lungs in quick, shuttering breaths as she scanned the room from where she lay on the floor in fetal position. She saw a bookshelf, three band posters, neatly-folded clothes, all vaguely familiar. She had to remember where she was, why she was here, why there would be—

Footsteps approached, hurriedly but softly, no shoes.

She leapt from the floor and wedged herself next to the bookshelf, where she was hidden from view of the door. As she and pulled her knees to her chest, she realized she was holding a book.

The door creaked open.

Greg's sketchbook.

Greg.

That was why she was here.

"Zarah?" whispered Bastian.

It flooded back to her, the heart attack, the hospital. She held her breath involuntarily, knowing in her mind that Bastian was not a threat, but in her body that he was the shooter here to kill her.

"Zarah," he said again, with an edge of concern. Bastian's silhouette formed in the dimly-lit room as he looked under Greg's bed. "Shit, where is she?"

She tried to remind her body that the shooter was killed on-site two years ago and this was Bastian and he was Greg's friend and he was worried about her and about Greg.

Bastian sat on Greg's bed and ran his hands over his face. "I should have warned—I didn't even think to tell Fred not to play that stupid damned game. He doesn't know."

Her breath caught in her throat. *Doesn't know?*

"There you are! Oh god, Zarah, I'm so sorry." He stood, and she wedged herself tighter against the bookshelf.

He held his hands up in surrender and sat back down. "I won't hurt you. I just…are you okay?"

She tried to speak, to ask him what he knew and how, why was he here, and what did it even mean to be okay, but the words all got stuck and came out as tears.

He knelt on the floor, hand still raised. "Zarah, I swear to you that I am Greg's friend Bastian, unarmed and here to help."

She shuddered.

"Should I call 9-1-1?"

"No," whispered Zarah.

"Are you okay?" he asked again.

Words came more clearly now to Zarah's mind as she considered the question. Was she okay? She was a paper filer with an almost-MA in History she'd never finish, who had finally let someone into her life who was a real, actual person and not a hamster or an imaginary superhero, but she'd let him lie dead on the floor after he'd had a heart attack. She made entire cakes for herself and had full conversations with people who weren't actually there. She didn't even know if the man who played guitar outside her window was real.

"No," she said.

"What are you feeling?"

The question seemed strange, but she thought about her answer. "Scared. Sad." As she said the words, her body loosened.

Bastian lowered his hands and began to crawl toward her. "What are you scared about?"

"The gunshots."

"What else?"

"Greg."

"What else?"

She sat normally now, no longer wedged. "I'm in a strange apartment with two guys I just met."

He laughed a little. "And what are you sad about?" He continued to inch closer.

"Greg."

"Me too. And?"

"And Iris."

Bastian reached out a hand to her. "Why are you sad about Iris?"

Memories filled her senses, Iris's easy laugh, the way her shoulders shrugged when she got excited over something silly, the floral smell of her shampoo, her hazel eyes lit over a new idea, the mental image of her eyes huge and wild with terror, mouth wide like in a horror movie—wider—screaming—tonsils—eyes dead and black hair thick with blood.

She was dead.

She couldn't be. She couldn't be, couldn't be dead.

But she was. She was dead she was dead she was dead and Zarah had let her die. If she'd just gotten off the fucking floor for once in her goddamned life! Zarah pulled on Iris's gold chain and looked at her Saint Christopher medal. SAINT CHRISTOPHER PROTECT US, it said. Iris had given Zarah her protection.

Zarah hadn't returned it to Iris's family. Hadn't gone to her funeral. Instead, she'd canceled her phone. Moved in with her dad. Never took off the medal, not even for showers.

Iris was dead.

Iris was dead.

Iris was dead.

Zarah fell into Bastian and clung to him as she sobbed. "I didn't mean it. I didn't want her to die. I want to go back. I need to. She can't be. She can't be."

Bastian reached his arms around her. "I'm so sorry, Zarah. I wish Greg was here for you."

Greg. Greg, whose stick-figure lifeless body had lain on the floor just like Iris's. Greg, whose body jumped as the paramedics brought him back to life.

She cried harder.

Bastian hugged tighter. "I can't help you with being sad or scared about what happened to Iris other than this. I'm here. I'm real. And Greggie's awake. He texted me."

Her heart leapt.

Bastian continued, "You don't have to come if you don't want to, he'll understand, but I'd be glad to drive you there if you want to see him."

She nodded into Bastian's chest, her breath shuddering.

"We need to bring his sketchbook and some comics. And booze and coffee."

Zarah pulled back and wiped her eyes.

"Apparently, his parents brought him a comic that is 'too mainstream'." Bastian rolled his eyes but smiled. "I'm not kidding. It's like taking Natty Bo to a beer snob's house."

"*The Indomitable X* is not Natty Bo," Zarah said as she caught her breath.

"You know what they brought him, then? Call it Yingling maybe. I don't know. I'll drink anything, personally." He stood and patted her shoulder. "Are you going to be okay?"

"No," she said confidently. "Everything's kind of fucked up right now."

"Amen to that," he said. "I'll round up Fred. Meet you in the living room in five?"

"Sure."

As Bastian walked out the door, Zarah leaned back against the bookshelf and breathed deeply. Greg was awake. She took stock of Greg's room, imagining him hanging his band posters, folding his clothes, sitting cross-legged on his gray comforter to sketch. Her heart ached for him to be there with her, to use giant hand motions to tell her about the time he saw his favorite band live, or how his mom taught him to fold clothes when he was a little boy, or how he made a graphic novel version of *Les Mis* for a school project. She hadn't the slightest idea if any of that were true, but her heart reached and reached and reached for him and his stories all the same.

No, she wasn't okay. But Greg needed her. And comics and his sketchbook—she could handle that. She could push through this.

She lifted herself to standing, brushed off her skirt, wiped the remaining tears from her face, and stepped around to the front of Greg's bookshelf. She was greeted first with hundreds of issues of Spider-Man. "And *The Indomitable X* is too mainstream?" she asked the bookshelf. She shook her head and ran her fingers over the two-inch thick spine of *Jimmy Corrigan*, off-beat, hefty enough for a hospital stay, but the sad story of a lonely man dealing with his broken family was probably not the best for someone who was already feeling sad and lonely. For a moment, she considered stopping by home for her favorite issue of *The Indomitable X*, issue 53, when X came to terms with the fact that he was never going back to his home planet. But no, she reminded herself to think of what Greg would want, not what she wanted him to read. She continued to wrack her brain as her eyes locked onto the spine of *Kris the Sad Rhinoceros*.

As if it were a preserved text, Zarah pulled the book off of its shelf and looked into the eyes of the rhinoceros on the front cover. What was making Kris the rhinoceros, Kris the human, so unhappy?

She opened to the first page, where Kris the smiling rhinoceros was playing in the watering hole with other animal children. One animal—Jake the zebra—was holding the rhinoceros's hand.

But on the next page, a baobab branch fell on Jake the zebra. Then Kris and the other animals crowded around Jake.

"Is Jake sleeping?" Kris asked her rhinoceros parents

on the next page.

"No, Jake died."

"But where did he go?"

"He lives in the stars."

"I'll take a rocket ship to him!" said Kris the rhinoceros, donning a pair of goggles.

"No, a rocket ship can't go that far."

"I'll call him on the phone!" said Kris the rhinoceros, brandishing a cell phone.

"No, they don't have phones in the stars."

Kris the rhinoceros frowned. "What can I do, then?"

As Zarah continued to page through the book, the rhinoceros family went outside to look at the stars. They talked about ways to remember Jake the zebra, about how to write him a letter, about having dinner with the zebra family because they were lonely, too. And on the last page, Kris the rhinoceros played with her friends under a zebra constellation.

Zarah closed the book and blinked at the back cover, where Morrow Maynard, Kris her boss, stared directly into her eyes.

Kris, who never smiled.

Kris, who galumphed around the office.

Kris, who wore nothing but gray suits.

Graham crackers. It was a fucking autobiography.

"Zarah," called Bastian as he poked his head in the door. "Did you find something for him?"

Zarah nodded as she slipped the book into Greg's messenger bag alongside his sketchbook.

CHAPTER 23

In the passenger seat of Bastian's Acura, Zarah carefully accepted a cup of drive-through coffee.

"According to Greggie," announced Bastian, "we are all three to pretend this is Turkish coffee."

Zarah nodded as the smell of slightly-burnt coffee reminded her of her days in DC, cradling a paper cup as she walked to the museum.

"Next up is you, Fred," said Bastian. "You said you have a near-empty bottle of Jameson at work?"

"It's Jack."

Bastian shrugged. "Cheap coffee and American whiskey will have to do for Al and Naomi for now."

"Those are Greg's parents?" asked Zarah, remembering suddenly that they, too, would be at the hospital.

"Affirmative," said Bastian as he turned onto Main Street toward the bar. "I didn't think about this being the first time you'll meet them. They're quite honestly the best."

Fred leaned up between the seats. "Bastian just says that because they were gonna let him move in if his parents disowned him for wanting to bang dudes."

"Thanks for including that detail, Fred."

"I'm just sayin'. You're not even their kid, so I thought it was pretty cool. My mom wouldn't't've."

"Fortunately, my parents did not, in fact, disown me for 'wanting to bang dudes,' but Al and Naomi are delightful, as you might expect of the two people whose genetic material created Greg Normand. They love everyone, so there's nothing to worry about, Zarah."

Nothing to worry about? She wondered why he would say that, single her out by name. Just because she had been hiding in a corner of Greg's room an hour or so ago while crying over video game sound effects, just because she had seen their son dead and then shocked back to life, just because their son had told her he loved her and then she had tried to take all his clothes off but still hadn't said it back until he was unconscious in the hospital—*Marathon*, there was *everything* to worry about.

"Here," said Fred as they pulled up to the bar. Bastian pulled over and put on his hazard lights.

"They even love Fred," called Bastian as Fred jumped out of the back seat.

Zarah glanced out the window and recognized the bar. She was only about a block from her apartment, steps away from X the hamster, from her own bed, from her collection of the Indomitable X comics, from isolation, from safety.

What would she even say to Greg's parents? What had Greg told them about her? What if she froze and the words never came out or she started crying because something about his mom reminded her of Iris or what if they recognized her Saint Christopher medal? What if they hated her because she was mute and strange and seemingly unfeeling, and Greg realized he could never be with her because his parents are "the best" and "love everyone" but they didn't love her?

"It'll be okay," said Bastian.

"I can't do it," whispered Zarah.

"We'll be with you, I promise. Greggie can't wait to see

you."

Zarah fought back tears as Fred re-entered the car.

"Please try," said Bastian. "But if you can't, he'll understand."

Zarah turned around to Fred and held out the coffee to him. "You take it. I can't."

"Wait, what?" said Fred, pulling back from the coffee.

"I have to feed my hamster."

"Feed your hamster?" Fred narrowed his eyes and mouth. "Fuck your hamster. You owe this to Greg. You have to go see him."

Zarah bit her lip.

"You've known Greg for what, two weeks?" spat Fred. "All we know about you is that you came onto our friend after he told you he loved you, but you never said it back. You're just a fucking whore."

Bastian retorted, but to Zarah his words were faded and distant as Fred's words echoed in her head. She was just a Medea or a Judas or a Vashti or any other betrayer's name because she was nobody and nothing. She didn't deserve a name. She wouldn't go to Greg when he needed her. She hadn't even stayed with Greg when he needed her. She hadn't resuscitated or helped or done a damned thing. She tried to summon some small fragment of Z in her soul, but she wasn't there.

Zarah gently placed the coffee in Bastian's cup holder and exited the car toward her building.

Zarah entered her apartment, lit orange by the setting sun, and let down what matted hair was left in her once-neat bun. After tossing her work clothes into the hamper, she changed into gym shorts and a tank top, some semblance of a regular evening at home with X the hamster. She stepped into her bathroom and stared into the cracked mirror, trying to envision herself as Z. The orange sunset painted fiery highlights on her red mane and spilled luminescence, like a squashed firefly, into the palms of her hands. Her eyes stayed locked on her image in the mirror as she pulled her hands through her hair and tried to imagine spooling light from it.

But instead she only saw a pale, quiet girl with smeared makeup whose greatest accomplishment was answering the office phone and greatest failings were enumerable and unspeakable. Her boring, human eyes blinked.

She wasn't Z, and was never going to be, because Z wasn't real.

Slowly, as if sleepwalking, Zarah stepped out of the bathroom. In front of her hung a poster of two dark eyes surrounded by yellow-white light with "The Indomitable X" written in block letters across the top. She looked into the Indomitable X's eyes and pulled down the poster, letting it fall to the floor like a giant dead leaf.

Then she moved into the kitchen, where the refrigerator held thirteen of the Indomitable X magnets, each of which she gently peeled off and let fall to the floor.

She removed the poster of the Indomitable X flying, of him slamming his fist down on Dr. Nemesinister, of him shining in a starry sky, of him standing atop the Eiffel Tower. He wasn't real and he was never going to be real any more than she was going to suddenly turn into Z. Greg wasn't the Great Gilgamesh or Jude or anyone but himself, because superheroes didn't need surgery. Superheroes didn't die on the cold, antiseptic exam room floor. Superheroes' bodies didn't twist and jerk and jump off the floor as electricity shocked their hearts back into beating. Superheroes didn't look frail as a stick figure underneath the scratchy blankets of a hospital bed. And superheroes didn't refuse to go to the hospital just because there would be strangers there.

No, superheroes didn't curl into fetal position when they should be doing CPR.

When they should be unlocking the door.

When they should be pulling Iris inside and barricading the door and calling 9-1-1 and saying, "It's over, it's okay, it's over."

Superheroes didn't leave their loved ones to die.

Zarah pulled on Iris's Saint Christopher medal and looked toward the ceiling. She tried to imagine Iris raging at her, punishing her, hating her for saving no one but herself. But instead, the sunset danced on the ceiling and painted iconographic Saint Iris, halo accented in gold leaf, fit to hang in a Greek Orthodox church. She held a key in one hand and extended the other as she gazed down on Zarah and smiled.

"I'm sorry," Zarah whispered, and weight escaped her like dandelion seeds lifting off in the wind. She reached up for Iris's hand and took it, gripping it lovingly. Feeling the solid warmth of her friend's hand, she wondered for a moment if she was sleeping or awake or had completely lost her mind, but Zarah decided she didn't care. "I miss you," she said to Iris. "I'm scared."

Saint Iris squeezed her hand.

"Iris, I don't know how to go on. I've been broken since…" She frowned and looked back at her room, where posters lay in piles like tornado debris and X ran furiously in his wheel. Her eyes snapped back to her white, empty ceiling and her own hand extended into the air, grasping nothing. "…since you died."

Familiar folksy guitar chords lilted up from the street below. Zarah heard Iris's voice singing, though she'd never heard her sing in real life.

We'll build a racetrack to the moon
Gonna get there soon
We'll build a racetrack to the moon with all our friends

Zarah stepped over to her desk and peered out her window. Down on the sidewalk, the Chordinator played guitar as Iris sang a song Zarah had written with Behnam in college.

We'll build a racetrack to the moon
And sing this little tune
We'll build a racetrack to the moon and marry Behnam

So Iris even knew the joke ending Behnam had written. Well, Iris didn't know it. Iris wasn't outside. No one was singing. *Right? Have I lost my fucking mind?*

Zarah looked at her laptop beside X's cage, thinking of weeks ago when she'd started to look for Behnam online. Maybe a dose of reality would do her good while her life was clearly in tatters.

Almost without thinking, she opened up her laptop and typed "B" into the search window. Her previous search of "Behnam" appeared, complete with pictures of Behnams who were not her ex-boyfriend. She hit the spacebar, thinking of their breakup over the phone, how she'd wanted to reach across the country and grab his hand, to understand how they could still love one another but didn't want to make it work. "S," and she could hear his laugh, like the laugh of a wheezing snake, as they commiserated over the pointlessness of chewing gum. "H," and he was in tears over his failed statistics final. "I," and he was standing on his bed, knitted lion hat on his head, singing songs from *The Lion King.* "R," and he was Roger from *Rent*; "A," and he was Johnny from *American Idiot*; "Z," and he was Elphaba from *Wicked*; "I," and he was—

On Facebook.

His picture was blurry, but his chestnut skin, his green eyes, his wolfish grin—they were unmistakably Behnam. He had his muscular arms around his brother and sister.

She clicked on his picture.

Your account has been deactivated. Reactivate?

She blinked at the screen. She'd deactivated her account after the internship, when she'd deactivated her phone. If she reactivated her account now—it was stupid. Why would she open herself up to the world again just to look at Behnam's profile? She wasn't even dating him anymore and she was falling for Greg and she needed Iris and he was neither of them but—

She clicked "Yes."

Her profile and picture appeared with a request to update both, and she was taken aback by the carefree smile across her sunkissed, extra-freckled face on the screen. It was like seeing the ghost of a friend who'd died long ago.

A notification blinked across the screen: *Benham Shirazi would like to video chat. Accept?*

Her heart leapt into her throat as her finger hovered over the mouse.

It prompted her again. *Accept?*

Fuck it, she thought as Iris's voice began to fade outside. She pressed "Yes."

Behnam's pixelated face formed on the screen, and its familiarity made her heart tear and grow with each beat. He had a beard and sported rectangular glasses instead of contacts, but his trademark smile spread across his face. "Zarah no-middle-name Smith." His voice made the time close in, as if it was two-and-a-half years ago and he was headed to dress rehearsal for a student-written play about Steve Wozniak. "Goddamn, I missed you," he said, shaking his head. "I didn't realize it until now. I figured you were just busy with your classes and your internship and—well anyway, did you know Facebook creepily notifies you if someone reactivates their account?"

"The Man's always watching," she said easily, as if she didn't have to try or think to talk, but the words came straight from her mind and out of her mouth without stopping to be processed and sorted and deleted.

"So what are you doing? Are you a curator yet?"

She shook her head. "Behnam, you know that takes years. But no. I honestly didn't even finish school."

He laughed. "Me either! Life got weird."

"No greater truth has ever been spoken," she said. "So I take it my idyllic image of you as an environmental lawyer taking down the Man by day and writing music with your wife and twin girls at night is far from reality?"

His mouth fell open before he burst into wheezing laughter. "Oh, hell. Totally wrong. Now I'm kind of ashamed to shatter your perception of my life."

"Behnam, I'm filing papers again at the doctor's office full time now. No need for shame unless you've resorted to actually being the Man. And even then, you'd probably be okay."

"Shit. What happened?"

Her heart ached. "I'd tell you it's a long story, but then you'd want me to sing you a damned ballad about it. So I'll just say it's a sad story. A really, really sad story. Not the kind I'm ready to tell."

"Not your dad?" he asked, face drawing into a frown.

"No, Dad's fine." She shrugged. "Just don't be afraid to tell me what you're doing now, because it takes hitting rock bottom to reactivate your Facebook account in the hopes of making human contact."

He frowned. "Well, I'll spare you the story and just give you the ending. The positive spin is that I'm following my dreams. The raw fact is that I made an impulsive decision and while I'm happy here, it's still kind of embarrassing."

"You're a porn star?"

"No! I would brag to the universe about that. No, I quit law school and moved to New York to scrape by on random gigs and share a studio apartment with three guys I met on Craig's List."

"Behnam! That's amazing!"

"Zarah, the abundance of body hair in that place is horrifying. Hence the reason I only go there to sleep. I'm in a coffee shop now. Yeah, I'm that guy. But hey, there's a reason I called you beyond wanting to catch up."

"Okay?"

"I've got an audition next week. And the song I'm singing, well, you'll understand when I tell you."

"What show?"

Behnam's grin faded to nervous tongue-biting. "Do you remember my dream role? Not Elphaba but the other one?"

The image of Behnam in his knitted lion hat, his 1997 *Lion King* poster, his bari-tenor voice belting Simba's songs flashed again in her mind. An easy smile spread across her face as she imagined him in a mask and full body makeup, roaring on the top of Pride Rock. "Of course I remember your dream to play Simba."

"I'm nervous as fuck," he said, pulling on his beard. "I'd been wishing I still knew you and could practice with you, and then your name popped up and I was like, it's fate. I've got to call her."

She looked at the guitar case jutting slightly from under her bed. "I wish I could help you, but I can't. I haven't touched my guitar in years. The strings probably aren't any good."

"Dear god, how sad is your story?" He paused. "I'm sorry, that was insensitive. Some fucked-up shit must've happened. I wish I had been there to help."

"No, really, it would have been too hard for you." She imagined him watching the news, panicking on the other side of the country as deaths mounted in the museum, missing all his classes and work and everything after it was over to carry her broken self through life. "But surely you know someone in New York, of all places, who can play you a couple chords? Or you could, I don't know, play them yourself?"

"It's not like that, though. I thought about some of the usual audition song choices and then realized, no, Simba's story is about losing everything and growing from hating and blaming himself for his father's death to proudly leading his people because it's the right damned thing to do. His songs are about both letting go of and embracing his past. So I thought, well hey, Zarah blew my mind a few years ago with the best song for that."

Her heart leapt into her throat for a moment. Losing

everything, hating and blaming yourself, letting go of and embracing the past: she should definitely know the song for that. That song was her life.

"Remember when you were singing in the hallway, and I literally cried because you touched my damned soul?"

She chewed on her lip, scanning the catalog in her brain for what he might be talking about. She'd thought she'd known pain in college. The pain of never having a mother, of breakups, of poor grades. But she'd known nothing. Nothing of real pain, of real hate and blame. How could she have known enough then to be able to sing a song like the one he remembered so clearly?

And then he began to sing.

At the sound of his warm but raspy first note, the dorm hallways constructed themselves around her, and she leaned against them instead of the back of her chair. Her hair was swept into a handkerchief, billowing and curly around her slender shoulders, as she finger-picked the notes to Florence + the Machine's "Shake it Out." It was a song about rising from your old self, about finding inner strength, about things she knew nothing about at the time she sang the song. Before she'd lost Iris. Before she'd lost herself.

She smiled, lyrics continuing to play in her head as she imagined Behnam as Simba. "You'll do a beautiful job."

"I know, right?" He chuckled. "Could you play it with me, Zarah? Help me practice? I mean, I'd say I'll repay you with a free place to stay here one weekend, but…"

"Body hair."

"Right."

She remembered exactly how to play the song, but to pull out her guitar again for the first time in front of Behn…

"I don't know. The guitar. I have trouble with music now." She paused and realized her apartment was silent. She peered over her laptop and no longer saw the Chordinator and Iris outside. "Let me think about it. I want to help you. And I want to tell you why I'm all fucked up. But I need a couple days. And I need to visit someone in the hospital and tell him I love him."

"Hospital? Shit, Zarah, I'm sorry."

"No, it's okay. This helped me. I just feel bad I'm not helping you."

"You are. You have. Take care of yourself, Zarah. I'd still give you the damned world, even though I know it would still never work for us."

"I'll call you soon, Behnam. And if I don't, call me. Here's my landline." She typed it in a message. "My lack of cell phone is part of the story. Thanks for this, Behnam."

"*Au revoir*, my dear," he said with a half-hearted wink.

The screen went blank.

Her apartment was still and silent. She gazed around at its empty walls.

"Shake it out," she sang into the emptiness.

The words hit the exposed brick walls and died like small birds.

What if…?

Her guitar case stared at her from its tomb under her bed. She slid out of her chair and crawled toward the case. Her hands shook as she pulled out the case and unlatched it with a ca-chunk, ca-chunk. Opening the lid, she beheld her curvy, wide-hipped Fender. Zarah ran her fingers over its polished wood, its old strings, like touching a lover who'd been presumed dead for the past two years, someone with whom she'd always had an understanding. Zarah crossed her legs, lifted the guitar by its neck, and held it in her left hand as she strummed with her right. She tuned it, string-by-string, half-expecting them to break. But the silk and steel strings sounded to her as pure as they had last she played in DC with her roommates, though she knew they weren't, really.

The strings cut at her fingers, but she moved deftly, though slowly, through the song she'd played so many times. As she picked up pace, she reached inside her guitar case compartment for a pick. But instead of a pick, her fingers grazed a cool glass surface.

Her stomach twisted and churned. Nausea tickled at her cheeks and lips.

Her cell phone.

She gently laid her guitar on the floor and peered inside the case's peripheral compartment. Her phone was nestled among various papers, like a nest for an egg. Lifting the phone, she remembered how it had been like an extension of her hand during her busy life in DC: directions, appointments, emails, phone calls. She remembered mounting it to her dashboard to direct her home after packing up her apartment. She remembered calling her dad to say she was on her way and realizing she'd become mute, unable to verbalize what had happened lest the words stick as truth. She remembered disabling the phone, locking it away.

She placed the phone on the floor next to her guitar. Then, one-by-one, she pulled out the papers forming the phone's nest: a receipt from the coffee shop that morning, a metro card, and an emergency line pamphlet from Officer Cortez. Sirens from the past blared in her ears.

"Call this number," Officer Cortez said over the sirens as he handed her an orange pamphlet. "There's a reference number inside. Fill out the left panel," he pointed to a checklist, "and let the nurse on-call know which of these items apply to you. They can't cover everything, but they can get you started."

Zarah had tucked the pamphlet into her purse, intending to call the next day after she'd had a chance to rest. And when the next day had come, she'd told herself again that she would call tomorrow. And tomorrow. And tomorrow. Weeks had passed, months, until one day she'd buried the pamphlet and everything else from that day in her guitar case. Everything except Iris's Saint Christopher medal.

Rubbing the medal now, Zarah opened the pamphlet and examined the checklist.

        Do you have nightmares?

Not really, she thought to herself with a sigh of relief, continuing down the list.

        Do you avoid situations,
        objects, or people that remind
        you of the event?

No, she thought, pressing her fingers into Iris's medal. *I wear this every day.*

        Do you avoid crowds?

Yes, but—

        Do you sometimes see, hear, or
        smell something that causes you
        to relive the event?

Not really until recently, right? It's not that bad usually.

        Do you lack positive or loving
        feelings toward other people and
        avoid relationships?

No! I have Greg. And I call dad once a month. And I talk to Franklin. And I just called Behnam. I'm getting better.

        Do you avoid seeking help
        because doing so keeps you from
        having to think or talk about
        the event?

Zarah blinked at the bullet as it echoed in her head. *Do*

I avoid seeking help because doing do keeps me from having to think or talk about the event?

Do I?

She looked over the list again. No, she didn't have nightmares. But she'd locked away her phone and her guitar and a receipt and a metro card for two years. She ordered groceries online to avoid being around other people. She filed papers in a back room, out of sight, never having re-enrolled in a Master's program. She didn't speak to any of her old friends. She barely spoke to her dad. She only spoke to Franklin because he didn't know her before, and if it wasn't for him, Greg would still just be a file on a shelf to her. And if it wasn't for Greg, she never would have had the nerve to call Behnam.

What did that mean, then? What was wrong with her? What would the nurse say to her? Would the reference number even work now after two years?

She shook her head and closed the pamphlet, feeling numb. "I need to sleep."

CHAPTER 24

Greg floated in the black vacuum of space. There were no moonlets, no mimosas from earlier. Only darkness.

Then, a flicker. A dim light shone in his chest for a moment, then faded. It flickered again, a heartbeat. Again. And again. And again. And then from his heart pulsated swirling planets, moonlets, asteroids, stars, galaxies, nebulae until the universe formed itself around him. He reached out to touch each piece of the universe, playing them like piano keys, and the music and the light and the vastness danced around him with life and love.

A hand squeezed his. Not a thin calloused one like his mom's or a cold one like his dad's, but a warm muscular handshake he knew to be his best friend's. Greg's eyes fluttered open to face Bastian leaning over him with a smile.

"Go back to sleep," Bastian whispered. "Fred and I sent your parents to the chapel so they could relax."

Greg blinked. *Chapel? Parents?* "Fuck," he muttered as his mind cleared.

"We're here for you," said Bastian. "We love you."

Greg glanced around the room, but from where he lay, he couldn't see around Bastian's large frame. *If my parents are in the hospital chapel, and Fred is here somewhere, then where is...* "Zarah?" Greg ventured.

"Zarah's not coming."

The world slowed to a stop as those words reverberated in Greg's head. Machines ceased beeping. Bastian's smile froze, emotionless as a mannequin's. Dust particles hovered in the air like the planets in his dreams.

Zarah's not coming.

She didn't love him. She couldn't. When she had so much of her own to deal with, she couldn't love a dying boy. She had to protect herself.

Gone was the image of her as a red-headed angel, of her whispering "yes" underneath him. Instead, she was the young woman from the newspaper, hurting and forever out of his reach.

She can't want me. She shouldn't want me.

His heart burned and tore and ached.

"Oh," he mustered in response to Bastian as the machined beeped again, as Bastian's smile faded, as the dust swirled and settled. Greg wondered if his heartbreak would show up on the monitors.

"She really wanted to." Bastian patted Greg's leg as he sat down next to him on the bed. Over Bastian's head, Greg could now see Fred standing in the corner, arms crossed. Bastian continued, "I...she...she's having a difficult time."

Of course she's having a difficult time. How is she going to break up with me when I'm literally dying? When we're not even dating?

"Greggie, you should call her."

Greg shook his head as unbidden tears stung his eyes. He was sick and he was dying and he was lonely, but he would damned well wait to fucking cry until he was alone.

"She loves you. I can tell. You need each other right now."

"Then why isn't she fucking here?" asked Fred. He uncrossed his arms and strode over to Greg's bed. "Explain it, Bastian, because I don't get it."

Bastian took a deep breath. "She was nervous about meeting your parents, Greggie. She's at home. You should call."

"It's not good enough," said Fred, face reddening. "Not for Greg. He's a fucking prince compared to her."

Bastian stood. "Maybe if you hadn't blasted video game gunfire in our apartment, I wouldn't have had to scrape her off the floor where she was sheltering in-place, and she would have been able to handle this. But you wouldn't know that, Fred, because you don't pay a damned bit of attention."

"Shh, stop," said Greg absently as his head swirled thinking of Fred playing *Band of Soldiers* and Zarah seeking shelter and *oh my God. Seeking shelter. Gunfire. Please no. She couldn't handle—*

His heart thrummed against his chest as he felt a wave of nausea and heat, imagining her huddled in a corner, eyes darting around the room as Fred slaughtered the masses on screen. Blood whoosh, whoosh, whooshed behind his ears as his vision faded.

Look what you did.

Me, it was you.

Greg. Greggie. Are you okay?

Fuck, fuck, fuck.

The room tilted and twisted like a funhouse. Greg closed his eyes.

The vastness of space was still there in his mind. The stars, the nebulae, all the pieces of the universe. He forced himself to breathe deeply through shuddering gasps. As he calmed, he noticed a tiny starburst of red floating among the pieces of universe. He swam over to it, and slowly a woman's shape formed, hanging limply. Zarah! He swam harder to reach her. She was cold, unresponsive. He held her close, his heart beating against hers, kissed her hair, sang to her that she was his red-haired queen. In the quiet after his song, he silently prayed to God and Saint Jude and Universe itself that they heal both of their hearts.

Greggie. Please. Stay with us.

The universe began to fizzle and pop like effervescence. He held tighter to Zarah.

Should we call the nurse?

The machines beeped quickly but steadily.

He looked down at his arms and realized he was alone in the universe, hugging himself.

Just stay with us long enough for your surgery tomorrow.

Ah yes, surgery. The surgery that his parents swore Saint Jude himself had made available to him. He felt the pinch of the IV in his hand, the pull of the electrodes on his chest. He opened his eyes.

"You're alive!" shouted Fred, who was grasping his hand.

Greg nodded, still seeing the outline of Zarah in his mind. He couldn't hold her. He couldn't comfort her from here in his hospital bed.

"Please just let us know what we can do to help."

Zarah. I need Zarah. But I can't have her.

"We didn't mean to upset you. We shouldn't fight in front of you. We're just so worried."

But what would I even say if I called her? "Hey, yup, having some surgery tomorrow, so come check it out and eat some snacks with my weirdo friends and my chapel-going parents"?

"We don't have a new comic for you, but you can read the one from your parents. Maybe that will help? I know you're a comic snob and everything but maybe it won't be so bad."

Greg blinked at the garish yellow TIX comic that Bastian held up. *What if I fucking read it?* he thought as Bastian handed it to him. *What if I actually fucking read it and call Zarah and surprise her and make her so happy that I chose to read TIX but oh my god what if it's the last thing I read on this earth and I die during surgery and my afterlife is shaped around the last thing that I read and I live in Rob Eager's mainstream sellout hell for eternity?*

"Your parents said you can't eat, or we would bring you ice cream."

You're being ridiculous, Greg. Remember what Dad said: Being an adult means that you try because no one else can do it for you. Read the comic. Call Zarah. Be an adult.

"Look, guys, I love you." Greg sighed. "But if I'm ever going to make it through the hell that is this day, I need like five seconds to myself without anyone shouting or crying or praying or stealing kids' art supplies."

"But—"

"Look. Give me enough time to read this horrendous comic, and I swear I'll call her. I swear to the Universe. Just give me some space to breathe."

Bastian grinned. "That's the spirit, Greggie."

Fred grumbled something about Justine as they walked out the door.

Greg closed his eyes and tried to allow his mind to clear, putting the surgery and his parents and Fred and Bastian and Zarah and every thought into a basket with baby Moses and letting them flow down the Nile, the way his mom had taught him to pray when he was a boy. But Zarah reached out from the basket, hair wild and curly, eyes brimming with tears. He pulled her to him and held her in his mind again as the rest of his thoughts floated away.

"If I can just see her," he said to himself as he opened his eyes. He stared at the Indomitable X, whose bright yellow body dominated the cover of the comic book he still held. In the bottom left corner, Dr. Nemesinister—*of all the damned ridiculous names*—lay flailing as TIX pressed a foot into his arch-enemy's throat.

"I can't believe she reads this nonsense," he said, shaking his head. "He's pure light," he mimicked a bubbly TIXer. "He's perfect in every way! He's big and he's strong and he's absolutely devoid of all flaws!"

"Well," he said, returning his voice to normal, "you're devoid of all emotion too, TIX. You know, it would be easier to be you. To have someone write me as this empty, emotionless alien who doesn't have a beating heart, so he can't have a heart attack." He glanced at his phone on the night stand. "Or a broken heart."

He sighed. "I'm not going to call her, am I, TIX? I know I said I'd read your comic, call Zarah, and be an adult. But am I really going to read this comic? Am I really going to call her? Or am I just going to sit here and talk to a figment of Rob Eager's imagination?"

He chuckled. "She'd laugh at me, you know. And she'd prod me. She'd say something that I would hate from anyone else but is so adorably genuine from her like, 'You just don't like X because he's unlike any superhero out there.' Like you're her douchey best friend she's trying to defend. And I'd be all like, 'You're right, he's not like any other superhero because other superheroes have souls.' And then she'd punch me in the shoulder and…"

Greg paused. "Why am I sitting here talking to a comic book when I could be talking to her?" He reached for his phone and searched for her number.

Call Zarah. Be an adult. Read the comic later. With her.

The phone rang. And rang and rang.

Dial tone.

"What?"

He tried again. It rang and rang. Dial tone.

"Something's wrong with my phone, right?" His voice cracked. His heart felt like it was splitting with each beat. Tears welled in his eyes. "I'm fucking dying, and she seriously can't even pick up her goddamned phone? She can't drive to the goddamned hospital?

"It's because she doesn't love you, Greg," he said to himself. "You always do this. You always love a girl and freak her out and why would she ever love you anyway? Why did your parents fly out to see you? Why did your friends come here? Because they feel like they have to? I'd rather they fucking didn't. I'd rather they be like Stacy Mills and just be honest and laugh at me. Just reject me. Just fucking reject me.

"Fred and his fucking stupid video games. Now she's gone. Gone! And I'm going to die here alone!" he shouted as he threw his phone at the door.

"Loud in here." The voice was a near-whisper from behind the door as it creaked open. The round, expressionless face that appeared was vaguely familiar, and as the door continued to open, he recognized Morrow Maynard.

"Your surgery is tomorrow," she said. "We need your authorization. We'll send paperwork."

Greg nodded, his self-deprecating thoughts knocked over by surgery coming back up the Nile on a speedboat.

"It will be okay," said Morrow, waving goodbye.

"Wait," said Greg.

Morrow remained unmoved.

"Zarah. You know Zarah. Do you think she'll visit me?" *What are you doing? You're grasping at straws, Don Juan. At dreams that will never be.*

"Yes."

"Oh. Really? Because I mean, I know this is, like, so much for her, and—"

"Yes." Morrow's mouth twitched into a half-smile for a moment before she left the room.

CHAPTER 25

Her eyes were closed, but she was awake. The ache of her heart felt almost like the remnants of a lingering nightmare, but it was just raw enough that she knew something real had happened, something she couldn't quite recall. And if she could just keep her eyes closed and refuse to remember, it would be like it hadn't happened. She knew this feeling well. It was Schrodinger's cat: it was at once alive and dead, real and not real, hovering in the blissful gray.

Her phone pierced the silence. And then she remembered. Last night, after she had gone to bed, the phone rang and rang but she was too paralyzed to answer. She had wondered if it was Greg, Greg, who'd had a heart attack. Greg, who most assuredly thought by now that she didn't really love him.

Then she remembered covering Lina's calls, the hospital, the video games, the flashbacks, the conversation with Behnam. It had all happened in one day.

The blissful gray burst into a turbulent sea of color.

She blinked her eyes awake, and as she looked around her room, she remembered she'd taken down all of her Indomitable X posters and magnets.

The phone stopped ringing.

X the hamster squeaked for a treat.

Zarah breathed deeply and ran her hands through her hair. She felt almost hungover, although she hadn't drank any alcohol. The emotions from yesterday churned and churned in her stomach, and she reeled for a moment as she stood out of bed. Carefully, she paced to her bathroom, where she stared at her haggard reflection in the mirror. She pulled at the puffiness of her eyes encircled by day-old smeared mascara. Her wild mess of curls reminded her of an unkempt lion's mane.

Returning to her bed, she stepped over her fallen posters, her guitar and case and papers and phone, murdered memories strewn about the battlefield of her apartment.

X the hamster squeaked again for a treat, and Zarah changed course instead to her desk. She slid into her desk chair and opened her heart-shaped box of sunflower seeds.

"I'm really broken," she whispered to X as she fed him, remembering the checklist the officer had given her. "I keep thinking I'm better, but I'm not."

Tears streamed down her face, as if leaking was the only thing her eyes were meant to do. She looked at her phone, guitar, receipt, metro card, and brochure. "I buried everything. And now it's dug up, and…" She rubbed Iris's Saint Christopher medal. "…and I guess I never really buried it in the first place."

She sat on the floor next to her guitar and pulled it into her lap. She pressed the wood against her heart and clumsily finger-picked her way through "Shake it Out," the notes still in her hands' memory but dampened and slow, fingertips burning with the cut of the strings without her old callouses. *Like me*, she thought, *raw without my old callouses. But I still know the way. Somewhere deep down.*

She closed her eyes and continued to work through the song, imagining each note pulling her real, raw, buried self forward.

"Z," she said aloud. She stopped playing and looked around her room. Of all the artwork, one superhero remained on her wall.

"The Others didn't bury Z, I did, and that's why her planet died. That's why Iris died. That's why Greg died." She thought of Greg alone in his hospital bed. "Am I going to let Greg die again?"

Her phone pierced her thoughts.

"Oh damn it," she said, standing and stepping to her desk. She picked up the phone. "Hey, hello, seriously, who keeps calling me?"

"Franklin, for fuck's sake," he grumbled.

She imagined the office forming around him. "Graham crackers. I forgot I had a job."

"Jesus. Well. I'm just calling to make sure you're alive. Which it appears that you are, despite your complete absence over the past fifteen or so hours."

"I was sleeping."

"Kris isn't here, but she insisted I call to tell you not to come in today. Which apparently wasn't on your agenda anyway, so that's encouraging."

"I'm going to go see Greg now," she said. Her heart leapt in her chest. "I guess now that I've said that, I have to."

"Yup, I'm texting him right now."

"Franklin!"

"What? He wants to see you. Let me give a guy some hope. Want me to drive you? You know your car's still here."

So much had happened over the past 24 hours that she'd completely forgotten. "Marathon's ass."

"What…who…you know what? Never mind. I'll pick you up."

"No, don't," she said, peering out her window at the low-grade crowd on the sidewalk. "It's five blocks. I'm walking."

"Oh shit."

"I'm living on the edge, Franklin. See you soon." Zarah hung up the phone and padded into the bathroom to wash her face. Thoughts orbited chaotically around her head but never quite touched her brain. *Z. Buried. Not buried. Greg. See Greg. Hide. Walk. Run. Stay with X. Go. Go! Go! Go!*

Greg's messenger bag greeted her by the door. "I'll be back," she said to X the hamster as she grabbed her keys and the bag.

As Zarah raced down her rusted staircase in flip-flops, she knew now was the time, if there was any, to summon Z. Avoiding Main Street, she cut through alleyways and ran her hands through her hair, trying to imagine her locks curling into ruby ringlets. But her fingers got stuck in the knots of her hair, and she nearly lost her balance as she tried to untangle them.

She stopped running. Freed her hands. Held out her palms.

She needed to be Z. She was everything Zarah hoped she could be but wasn't. Z was a hero bursting down a door and saving everyone instead of hiding in fetal position. Z's heart was bold and shining and bright. Z's hands were ripe with bolts of electricity, of all the power she needed to save earth. And she'd been fucking buried all this time.

She needed to unbury Z.

But Zarah's hands were pale and mortal and wrapped in broken pieces of hair.

Because Z's story wasn't real. Z wasn't real.

Zarah sat down in the alleyway, next to a trash can.

Z wasn't the fictional embodiment of truth, like Zarah had postulated of the heroes in her unfinished thesis. Z was just a lie, a lie she'd created so she could sleep, so she could get through life without cracking, without always hiding, without starving and dying of grief. Zarah had formed the lie of Z, crafted her from pieces of her own soul.

She kicked the trash can.

You're burying her again, she thought.

I crafted Z.

I created her.

I made her.

Zarah looked again at her hands, the broken hairs tumbling off in the summer breeze.

I made her.

One hair flew back into her face, tickling her nose.

I'm real.

The thought surprised her.

I'm real.

I tickle.

I hurt.

I'm real.

I'm not the quiet, mousy alter-ego. I'm the real one.

And Z? I made her. I made her out of my soul. Z is part of me. Part of my mind. Part of my psyche. Part of who I am. Z isn't buried.

Z is me.

"I am Z," she whispered to herself as she stared at her human hands, knowing that her power didn't come from flawless ringlets.

"I am Z," she proclaimed to the alleyway, the apartment buildings, the trash cans.

So what if I don't have superpowers, she thought as she stood. *If I don't have a sparkling complexion. If I don't have fans or magical friends. I'm Zarah Smith. I'm not Greg's Zarah. I'm not Behnam's Zarah. I'm mine. I survived. I'm here. And damn it, I'll be there for Greg.*

With renewed courage, Zarah stepped toward Main Street, hands at her sides. She didn't need to run her hands through her hair or rub Iris's medal. As she approached the sidewalk, she watched skateboarders and strollers and dogs and joggers move as one. She hesitated, about to turn back. But she closed her eyes. "I am Z," she whispered again, and she opened her eyes to see not a crowd but individual people, people who looked to heroes to save them, people who—yes—could be just as afraid of her as she was of them. As if diving into water for the first time, she merged into foot traffic and began jogging as one of the crowd.

CHAPTER 26

Zarah strode through the hospital's revolving doors with all the purpose of an Olympic powerwalker and jogged down the hallways, following signs for intensive care, picking up speed, rounding corners, getting closer and closer to his room until she went careening into a cluster of pink balloons.

Zarah nearly fell back as the balloon cluster dissipated to reveal Kris in her usual gray suit. Zarah's office manager looked up as 20-something pink balloons congregated on the hospital ceiling.

In the emotional upheaval of last night, Zarah had forgotten Kris's book, the story of a rhinoceros who had suffered a traumatic loss and forgotten how to smile. And for the first time, instead of seeing the Rhinocerkris, Zarah beheld Morrow Maynard: a broken human being who had thought to bring balloons to the hospital but erred and bought far too many to be socially acceptable, her last 20 shreds of sanity bouncing on the ceiling.

"Here, I'll help you." Zarah pulled down a balloon and handed it to Kris, who blinked at her mutely.

Zarah gathered more balloons. Pink. They were all pink. Baby Scarlett! "These are for Lina, aren't they?"

asked Zarah as she handed Kris a handful of balloons.

Kris nodded.

"That was nice of you," she said as she handed Kris the last balloon. "Tell Lina congratulations. I'm actually here to see…"

"Mr. Normand."

"Yes."

Kris crinkled her eyebrows and pursed her lips as she studied Zarah, the way someone would scrutinize a cliff's edge before bungee jumping.

"Here," Kris finally said as she reached into her suit pocket and produced a business card.

Zarah read the card.

Dr. Lawrence, Licensed Therapist.

Zarah's heart accelerated. Her temperature rose.

"I saw the news two years ago," said Kris as Zarah continued to stare at the card. "Senseless," she spat. "It always is. But things can only get better if you let them."

Zarah remembered walking into Kris's cat-adorned office three years ago to ask for a letter of recommendation. *Opportunity in DC: Museum of Ancient History.* And then the shooting. And from her dad's living room, Zarah had emailed Kris asking to return to her old job, to which she was met with one word, "Yes."

"I've been seeing Dr. Lawrence for ten years," continued Kris. "She can help you if you're ready."

Kris hadn't hovered and lurked because of mistrust; Kris knew.

Kris gives a fuck.

When Zarah looked up, Kris had already galumphed away.

Greg's room was brighter than it had been yesterday afternoon, with flowers and balloons on the windowsill. Greg was propped up in bed with his face hidden by the latest issue of *The Indomitable X*. Zarah's heart leapt. On the front cover, X stood with his sunny foot on Dr.

Nemesinister's throat, Dr. Nemesinister gasping and reaching but unable to spar with light itself. In true Rob Eager fashion, the back cover depicted the reverse, with Dr. Nemesinister's pristine black leather boot on X's neck as X thrashed in vain hope. Yes, she thought, this was a wise issue to start him on, one that capitalized on the power struggle between the mortal enemies which had become deadlocked in recent issues, finally abolishing any hope surrounding their glimmer of mutual understanding found in issue 97.

Greg peeked over the comic and smirked. "Okay, so I guess I can see where you're coming from," he said as he put the issue in his lap, as if Zarah had been there the whole time. His glasses were straight now, his cheeks less pallid, his eyes fully open. "TIX is legitimately kind of badass. But—before you get too excited—I still think this guy's pompous as hell. I mean, he just calls himself by a letter."

She wanted to run to him, to hold him, to tell him—

"Please explain your fascination to me, Zarah."

You're reading my favorite comic, she wanted to say. *You're upbeat even when you're in intensive care. You fly drawings around my room and make up theme songs and bring both our imaginations to life in your sketchbook. You draw faceless angels and desperate people and you breathe life into all of the broken pieces of my life. That's my fascination. That's why I love you.* But instead, she looked at Greg's eyebrows, raised in expectation of an answer to his actual question, and she ventured, "He's X because he's undefinable."

He shrugged. "Then maybe his name should just be, like, white space on the page. Like Rob Eager should just leave a space."

"That wouldn't make any sense."

"Not any more sense than 'X.'"

She stepped closer and sat next to him on the bed. "Then what about Z?" She let her hair, tangled though it was, drape over her shoulder. "You don't seem to have a problem with her name just being a letter."

"What problem could I ever have with Z?" He hesitated, then ran his fingers through her curls. "She's a damn sight cooler than TIX. Not even in the same league." The corners of his amber eyes creased. His smirk faded. "You didn't come to see me last night."

Her heart sank. "No."

"I know, I mean *I know* that it was all too much. Bastian told me about the video game and—well I don't make you want to relive it again, but—I mean, it was a really shitty day for both of us, right?"

She nodded.

"I'm not mad now that you're here. But I was yesterday. I was mad because I want this to work. Whatever this is. I don't want to say I need it to work, but sometimes I think I do, and then I wonder if maybe that's just because I'm sick, and—"

"I came here to tell you I think I love you, too," she whispered.

He ran his thumb along her cheek, and she felt every unspoken word pass through their silence.

She leaned over to kiss him, lips barely touching. She opened her mouth, touched his tongue with hers as he cradled her face in both his hands, felt her heart beating hard in her chest as she wanted to grab him and have him and say every word to him that she'd been thinking, but her nose caught on his oxygen tubes and his heart monitor beat faster and they both started laughing.

"Well," Greg said, scratching the back of his neck, "I'm glad we, you know, did this because I'm having surgery in, like, a few hours."

"What!"

"Okay, so, according to my parents, this was Saint Jude's doing, but actually your boss scheduled me as soon I went code blue in the office because, apparently, that was kind of traumatic for folks and I guess fixing me up quickly is good press. Or at least better press than a dead

20-something on the office floor."

"I actually quite literally ran into Kris on my way here."

"I'm scared, Zarah," he whispered. "They're going to like, zap my heart and literally kill part of it. I mean, it's the broken part, but still."

She put her hands on his face. His skin was cool and clammy. "I remember when you were just a file in the office," she said. "A file with a funny name. Gilgamesh. And now you're you. You're Greg. And I love you."

He grinned. "Somehow, that's the only thing that could make me feel less terrified. I love you too, Z."

She grinned. "I realized on the way here that I am Z, after all."

"Of course you're Z. You always have been."

A gentle knock sounded on the door. "Greggie?" said a woman's audio-book-worthy voice.

Greg's eyes widened and he gripped Zarah's shoulders. "So those are my parents," he whispered.

She leapt out of the hospital bed and nearly fell, catching herself on the nightstand. His parents? The perfect ones? The ones who loved everyone except probably her?

"Mom! Dad!" called Greg. "Give me, like, five minutes."

"It's okay," whispered Zarah. "Unless I shouldn't meet them."

"No, no! It's not that. I just don't want to overwhelm you, and—"

"Okay, sweetie!" called Greg's mom.

"Wait," said Zarah as she walked toward the door and opened it. In front of her stood a tall Black woman with a halo of dark, tightly-curled hair like Greg's, next to a wiry white man with glasses and gray hair.

"Zarah," said the man with his arms extended for a hug.

Zarah stepped into the embrace, and while the man's physique was completely unlike that of the Indomitable X, a similar warmth of Christmas Eve by the fireplace ran through her body as she tentatively reached her arms around him. She thought of her own father, how she barely spoke to him anymore. How she barely spoke to anyone. How, in reality, she wasn't that unlike Kris.

Greg's mom rested a hand on Zarah's shoulder. "Thank you for loving our Greggie," she said.

"Mom!"

Zarah laughed. "Of course," she said, stepping out of the hug. "I'll give you guys some time."

"No, Zarah, stay," said Greg.

Zarah fiddled with Greg's messenger bag she still wore, remembering tucking away Kris's therapist's business card the way she had tucked away the emergency hotline brochure two years ago. She'd call tomorrow. But—tomorrow would become tomorrow and tomorrow and tomorrow. And Greg wanted to make this work. So did she. And if it was ever going to work, she needed a doctor the same way he did.

"I'd love to," she said. "But I need to make a phone call. I'll see you before surgery."

"But you don't have a phone," said Greg. "Borrow mine."

"Joan's going to call you," said his father, reaching in his pocket. "Here's mine, Zarah. I'm sure we'll see you again."

"Thanks," she whispered as she stepped out the door. She walked in a daze in the hallway, Dr. Lawrence's business card in one hand and Greg's father's cell phone in the other. Both shook in her hands. How could she summon an actual voice to reach out for the help she knew she needed but hadn't the strength to obtain?

The past twenty-four hours were still a blur. Lina had her baby. Greg had a heart attack. Zarah played video games with strangers and played the guitar and talked to Behnam and even answered the phone at the office and talked to strangers.

The phones. She remembered Angie's advice, "Write a script. It helps."

Zarah continued through the hallways until she found a bench by a window overlooking the hospital garden. She sat down and rummaged through Greg's bag for a pencil. On the back of the business card, she wrote out her script.

Ready to dial, she caught a glimpse of her face in the reflection of the phone's screen. She was weary. She was pale. Her hair was matted. It had only been twenty-four hours, but she was still here. She was still alive. And she was Z.

"Of course you're Z," she said aloud, echoing Greg's words. "You always have been."

She unlocked the phone and turned Dr. Lawrence's business card back to the front. She just had to press the numbers, one by one.

That first number was the hardest. Seven. Fucking seven.

Just press seven.
Z could press seven.
Z would press seven.
And you are Z.
I am Z.

The tone sounded as she pressed the number. And then the next. And the next and the next, until she was calling Kris's therapist just like she had searched for Behnam's name. Just like she'd pressed "call" to talk with Bastian. Just like she'd read from a script to talk with patients.

A disembodied voice spoke to her on a recording, asking her to leave a message. She turned over the business card and read her script.

"Hello, my name is..." She paused. "I'm Zarah. Also Z. They're both my name. And I'd like to make a new patient appointment."

CHAPTER 27

The whir of the noise cancellation machine filled the silence between Franklin and Zarah as they sat in the sole two chairs in Dr. Lawrence's waiting room two weeks later. He'd offered to drive her—in his Franklin way—when she'd mentioned it that morning: "Well, someone needs to make sure you don't just sit in your car like a big weirdo, pretending you had an appointment."

Now, Zarah shifted in the blue upholstered chair, staring at a painting of sunflowers on the wall. She recognized it as one of Van Gogh's, the mustard-colored flowers wilting in a yellow and white vase. Zarah wondered why a therapist would choose dying flowers painted by a man who committed suicide to greet her patients. "Did you know?" she asked Franklin.

"That you like peanut butter and jelly sandwiches? No, but I'd assumed so."

She turned her head to meet his grin next to her. "Franklin, be serious."

"I am serious! Peanut butter and jelly…" he trailed off as she frowned at him.

"Did you know that I'm—" she hesitated. The shape of the word *crazy* caught in her mouth and chained her to the chair.

"You're the sanest person in our damned office," Franklin said matter-of-factly.

"But did you know about what—what happened to me?"

He shook his head. "No. But I could tell something must have happened."

"How?"

"There's a tentativeness about you. That's why I took you out for lunch the first day we met. Plus, I'd heard that you'd been working on your Master's degree and suddenly came back to filing papers." He looked at his hands as he wrung them together—a gesture that was so un-Franklin that Zarah felt frozen in the moment. "I know sadness," he said. "It sucks. But it helps to have someone else who gets it, even if you never talk about it." He paused and looked back at her. "I've never been brave enough to do this, though. I'm really proud of you."

Before Zarah could respond, the door opened, and a young woman in a red tank top and holding a baby walked out, avoiding Zarah's and Franklin's eyes. Zarah thought again about Lina, how she hadn't called her or congratulated her, and the weight pulled at her heart.

Dr. Lawrence emerged. She was older—maybe in her 60s—and held her gray hair up with a pencil. She had kind, pale blue eyes with eyelashes so thin she could barely see them. "Zarah," she said, holding out her hand. "I'm Katherine. Nice to meet you."

She stared at the woman's hand.

Franklin gripped Zarah's shoulder. "That's you, kid," he said. "Zarah Smith, nerd extraordinaire."

The heaviness around Zarah shattered at Franklin's touch, and she reached up and clasped her hand over his before standing and shaking Dr. Lawrence's— Katherine's—hand.

As she followed Katherine, Zarah's eyes darted around the office at the fluffy white area rug, the green couch, the mobile of origami cranes hanging from the ceiling, the seashells and rocks on the wall-length windowsill. Zarah stepped toward the window and looked out at the Rocky Mountains, reddish brown and indigo in the distance.

"Tell me about yourself, Zarah," said Katherine in the calm voice of a yoga instructor. Zarah turned around to face her. The therapist was now sitting in an office chair, notepad and pen in-hand.

Zarah picked up one of the seashells from the windowsill, a tan scallop the size of a quarter, and rubbed her thumb over its ridges as she considered the question. Where could she even begin?

"You're welcome to have a seat on the couch, if you'd like. Or you can look out the window. However you're comfortable. And please, bring the shell with you. That's why they're here."

Zarah stared at her shell. Iris had always loved the ocean. Talked about how she used to swim with her sisters.

But now Iris was dead.

"So Zarah, what were you doing before you came here?" asked Katherine.

"I was working," Zarah said, thankful to stop thinking about Iris. "I file papers at a cardiologist's office."

"And how long have you worked there?"

"Nine years. Off and on. I worked summers and breaks during high school and college. But I've been full-time two years."

"And how do you like that?"

Zarah traced a swirl of dark brown on the shell. "I mean, it's filing papers. It's okay, I guess."

"And what about the man who was waiting with you outside? Who is he?"

"My co-worker, Franklin."

"Tell me about Franklin."

"He's funny." Zarah looked up at Katherine, who sat poised on her chair, eyebrows raised, nodding for Zarah to continue. This sort of small talk was somehow easy in this room, with someone Zarah wasn't meant to impress or who would generally require her to appear *normal*. "We met two years ago," Zarah continued, "when I started full-time. He's training me to perform electrocardiograms because eventually all our files will be digital, and I won't have this job anymore. But that means I need to interact with patients."

"How do you feel about that?"

"I'm getting used to it. But I don't really like people."

"Do you like Franklin?"

"Well, yes."

"Is there anyone else at work who you like?"

Zarah looked back out the window. Marathon, she didn't really know anyone well enough to actually like them. Except—"Lina. She just had a baby. We used to be friends. Until..." Zarah trailed off and traced the mountain range with her eyes. She knew that this was why she was here—to talk about what happened at the museum. But the words just...were living somewhere on Pike's Peak, 8000 feet of altitude out of Zarah's reach.

"Let's come back to that. Is there anyone else outside of work who you like?"

Zarah laughed as Greg's wide smile overtook her mind's vision. "Greg. He's the first boyfriend I've had in almost three years." As she said this, the word "boyfriend" felt almost silly on her lips, like it was something reserved for a teenager. But was he really a "partner" after just a month? Even given all they'd gone through together?

"How long have you and Greg been dating?"

The conversation continued for another fifteen minutes through how they'd met, Greg's heart attack, his surgery, the fact that he was home and recovered now. As Zarah talked, she walked toward the green couch, eventually sitting down.

"What about your family?" asked Katherine.

"I don't have much family." Zarah shrugged. "It's

always just been me and my dad. No siblings. Dad never talked about my mom."

"Where is your dad now?"

"He's in Montana. I lived with him for a little while after the—" she paused. Zarah felt the memory spiraling in her mind. But instead of shoving the memory back into its bottle, she let it wash over her.

Crack!-Crack!-Crack!

High-pitched, blood-curdling screams erupted outside the Mesopotamia storage closet. Indistinct shouting. Pounding feet. Shattering glass.

The doorknob convulsed.

Zarah dove behind a pile of tablets. Shivering, she curled into the fetal position and tried to breathe, but her lungs were paralyzed.

Crack!-Crack!-Crack!

"Parakalo, Zarah, let me in!" cried Iris on the other side of the door.

Crack!-Crack!-Crack!

Zarah's heart pounded so hard she thought it was crushing her lungs. Everything sounded underwater.

"Please!" Iris's voice. "Oh God! He's killing us!"

Zarah pushed the muscles of her arms, shouting with the force, but she was paralyzed as her heart beat harder and harder and her vision blurred and—

Crack!-Crack!-Crack!

"He's coming!" Iris cried, her voice guttural, visceral. She thudded against the door. "Zarah, he's coming!"

MOVE! MOVE! PLEASE! Zarah screamed at her arms, her legs, her useless body locked in fetal position.

"Páter imón, o en tois ouranoís—"

CRACK!

Slump against the door. Pounding feet. Silence.

Shuddered breaths. Shaking.

No it couldn't it couldn't it couldn't.

No.

Waiting.

Waiting.

Footfalls.
Pounding.
Open the door!
So cold. Can't move.
Pounding. OPEN THE DOOR!
OPEN THE DOOR!
OPEN THE DOOR!
Nightmare. Paralyzed. Help me.
Ratting doorknob. Latch clicking.
HANDS IN THE AIR!
But she didn't move.
You're safe now, ma'am.
Just a few questions.
Follow me.
Can't move.
Being carried, shoved.
Bodies.
Blood.
An elderly couple.
A man and his two kids—children for fuck's sake.
Iris's dead eyes.

Zarah sat on the therapist's couch, drenched in the memory, in her tears, in sweat. She had drawn her knees to her chest and begun rubbing Iris's medal.

"Something bad happened two years ago." Zarah's voice cracked. "So I've been pretending I'm someone else. Pretending it didn't happen. But I've been remembering."

Katherine's countenance remained unchanged as she handed Zarah a box of tissues. "When did you start remembering?"

After her appointment, Katherine scheduled Zarah for a visit every Wednesday for the next month. "We'll meet weekly for awhile, Zarah. Until next week, I have one thing I want you to do for me: I want you to explore Z by writing her story, drawing it, or composing music for it."

Zarah thought about Greg's sketch of Z and the way

he flew it around the apartment. She thought about her guitar and Behnam. "Can I work with someone else?" she asked.

"I think that's a wonderful avenue to explore," said Katherine. She held out her hand. "It was nice to meet you, Zarah. I will see you next week."

--

Greg sat cross-legged on his bed, sketching the 300-foot-tall reddish brown sandstone formations of the Garden of the Gods. Some reached for the clouds like eroding columns and others formed triangular walls like two waves crashing into each other—all against the backdrop of the mountains. At the rocks' base stood Jude, wings and arms outspread as if to embrace the natural wonder. Next to him, Z shot lightning into the clouds overhead, illuminating the skyline.

After his surgery two weeks ago, Greg's parents had stayed at a nearby hotel while he'd recovered. Dr. Desai said he'd be fine, but they insisted on staying a whole week. "We'll get some sightseeing in," Greg's dad said. So after Greg had been home three days and cleared for "normal activity," Bastian piled them all into two cars and led a trip to Garden of the Gods.

"It's like an outdoor cathedral," Greg's mom said as they stepped out of their cars.

"Why does everything have to be about church with you and Dad?" Greg joked, but honestly, he agreed with his mom. It was as if great giant gods had all kept a rock garden before they ascended to the heavens, leaving it behind as a place of worship for their devotees.

"You could baptize a baby right over there, Al," Bastian said, pointing to a square-shaped rock about three stories tall, balanced precariously on another.

"Or Greginator could get married on those kissing rocks," Fred joined in.

"Good lord," Greg muttered, but then his parents each put an arm around him, flanked by Bastian and Fred. And under the warmth of all their arms, facing the stillness of the park and the vastness of the formations and mountains, Greg had known that no matter what happened with Zarah or the comic book store or his heart, he was okay in that moment.

Back in the present, someone rapped on Greg's open door. He looked up to see Zarah in a bright yellow dress. At the sight of her smile, his body felt warm again the way it had in the Garden of the Gods, but with a quickened pulse and rush of blood to his cheeks.

"Hey," he said. "I didn't know you were coming over today."

Zarah shrugged and walked over to his bed. "I wanted to see you. What are you working on?"

"Um."

"Oh, Garden of the Gods!" As she sat next to him, their bodies touched casually as if Zarah had been coming over every day for the past year. Her eyebrows raised as she looked at his sketch. "Greg, this is stunning. I've never seen Colorado in a comic book before, at least not like this."

"Yeah, big cities get all the love." He watched her continue to gaze at his drawing, her eyes tracing the natural skyline. *Do I ask her about therapy? Is that weird? She seems happy, but—*

She grasped his hand and met his eyes. "Can you help me explore Z's story in comic form? It's homework. For therapy."

"Um, sure. So therapy went okay, then?"

"Yeah. It was hard, and part of me wanted to go back to my apartment and hide with X, but another part of me was afraid that if I did that, I'd never come back out." Zarah looked at their intertwined hands. "I know we met each other at a weird time. For both of us. And I know we've gone through too much to start over. Not that we need to. But it does mean that if this—" she squeezed his hand "—is going to work, you're going to be along for the ride. It's not your responsibility, but…"

"Zarah," Greg said as he tucked a loose curl behind her ear, "I have a notebook full of ideas for *Jude vs. the Universe* that have never materialized into more than just random scenes. But since I met you, I've seen Z shooting lightning out to all those disparate parts, connecting them, weaving them together into something new: *The Adventures of Jude and Z.*"

"But Z's story is sad," she said.

"Every superhero's story is sad." He held her face in his hands. "That's the only way to become great. To refuse to let life crush you."

"But hers…mine…" She trailed off and looked away from him.

He grasped her shoulders. "Zarah, you never have to tell me what happened. You can if you want, but that's never something I expect of you. We're broken. We're fucked up. We can't fix each other. We can't make each other whole. But I want you there while I figure out what piece goes where in my life."

She pulled his hands from her shoulders and held them in her hands. "That's what I want, too."

CHAPTER 28

Two months later, Zarah clung to her tablet with one hand as she peeled an electrode off Ms. Long's chest with the other. "I'm not qualified to tell you the results," Zarah read from her tablet. "But Dr. Desai will be right in, and she'll explain the results to you."

"You can't give me...some idea of what she'll say?" Ms. Long asked as Zarah continued removing electrodes.

"I'm afraid I can't." Zarah knew the script well, almost had memorized it over the past two months. But today, she paused to look into Ms. Long's worried eyes and imagined she were in her place, heart fluttering, legs swelling, and smiled. "Don't be afraid," she said off-script. "I've seen Dr. Desai save lives. She'll know just what tests to run."

Ms. Long looked down at her folded hands.

Zarah bit her lip. "Just think about chocolate cake," she said quickly.

Ms. Long looked up and raised an eyebrow

"With sprinkles, of course." She shrugged. "It seems to work for most people."

Ms. Long chuckled. "All right, I suppose I can wait for the doctor."

Zarah threw away the disposable electrode pads and removed her gloves. "She'll be right in."

As she closed the exam room door behind her and walked down the hall, she smiled to herself. She'd been a full-time EKG tech for a month. Although she'd clung to her tablet at first, never speaking a word off-script, she realized over time that most patients were even more nervous than she was.

Zarah cleared her thoughts, took a deep breath, and knocked on the door of Exam Room 2 before entering. On the exam room table sat a familiar young man with glasses and big, beautiful hair.

He looked her up and down and shook his head with a laugh. "Where did you find TIX scrubs?"

"The internet, of course," she said, pulling on new gloves.

"I, um, brought you some peach rings." He tapped the paper bag next to him as she stuck the electrodes to his chest.

"You are entirely too kind."

"You know, I'm proud of you, Zarah. I never thought I'd see the day when you'd willingly talk to strangers for eight hours a day."

She stuck the last electrode to his chest and shrugged. "I'm still using notes, though. It's not like I really talk to them."

Greg grasped her shoulders before she could start the EKG. "But that's a huge deal, Zarah. The first time I met you, you literally ran away from me. You've been working so hard with Katherine. And remember what she told you? That you might have to always work harder than everyone else. But you're Zarah, and that's what you're doing. Let yourself be proud."

She grinned. "I *am* kind of proud of myself."

"Good," he said, releasing her. "So, for tonight, I've got tons of new sketches from just, you know, sitting in the waiting room. The latest one," he said, waving his hands in front of him as if he were finger-painting on the air, "is of Jude finding Z unconscious in Purgatory, USA. And she seems all helpless and limp, but when she wakes…well, I guess I should surprise you later."

"Greg! Not fair!" She started the machine.

"Not fair? You hold all the power. I don't know what you're going to do with those gloves or that machine. I'm sitting here half-naked and you're all covered in scrubs. That's what's not fair."

She shook her head. When the test ended, she glanced at the results, and though she wasn't qualified to provide them to any patients, a combination of Franklin's training and the online class she'd been taking assured her that the waves of Greg's heart likely indicated normal results.

Someone knocked at the door. "Better be keeping it professional in here," said Franklin as he stuck his head in. "Oh. I'm mildly disappointed that you are."

Zarah playfully rolled her eyes. "Graham crackers, Franklin. I ran the test. Greg's ready for Dr. Desai."

Franklin shook his head at her scrubs. "Seriously, what the hell is on her outfit, Greg? Please don't tell me it's weird comic shit."

"The worst kind," said Greg.

Franklin sighed and turned toward the door. "Damned comics," he muttered as he started to exit the exam room. "Oh and Zarah," he said, peering back in. "Lina and the baby are here—they're waiting for you in the file room. I'll cover your next patient."

Zarah's heart quickened as she approached the file room. As part of her therapy, Zarah had emailed Lina last week to congratulate her on baby Scarlett. Even though Zarah had been worried that Lina wouldn't reply or might be mad that Zarah had shut her out these past two years, Lina had responded a few days later with pictures of her and a wrinkled little baby with closed eyes and scratches of black hair.

Now Lina stood amidst the file shelves—which were now empty from the move to digital—rocking a bundle of blankets with rainbow ducks on them. Lina looked up from shh-ing the fussing baby and smiled. "Zarah!"

"Lina!" Zarah said, walking close and peering into the blankets at baby Scarlett. The baby blinked at Zarah and grumbled.

"How are you feeling?" Zarah asked Lina.

Lina, who usually wore Pinterest-worthy eye makeup, had circles under her eyes and a bare face. Her smile seemed tired but genuine, the way Zarah remembered her dad looking at her when she was young. "She doesn't sleep more than two hours at a time," said Lina. "But Barry is helping." She continued to bounce the baby. "Do you want to hold her?"

Zarah thought for a moment. She'd never held a baby, nor ever wanted to hold one. She didn't know where to put her arms or how to bounce the baby. But this was Lina's daughter.

"Here," Lina said, holding out the bundle. "Just crook your arms like this." As she talked, she held the baby to Zarah's chest, and Zarah shaped her arms around the baby. Lina pulled her arms out, and Scarlett rested in Zarah's arms. The baby was warm, and heavier than she had expected. Scarlett wriggled as she gazed up at Zarah.

Zarah stood like a statue, afraid that with the slightest movement, she'd accidentally drop this tiny human.

"You're doing great," said Lina. "Hey, did you ever get an appointment for that patient you asked me about? Did Kris have an opening?"

As Zarah thought through what appointment Lina might be talking about, Scarlett reached her tiny fingers out from the rainbow duck blanket and made an "ah" sound before she started chewing on her hand. *Greg*, Zarah remembered. "I did," she said in a sing-songy voice as if talking to baby Scarlett. "I found Mr. Normand an appointment. He's better now." She looked at Lina and spoke in her regular voice. "It's actually kind of a wild story. I'd love to catch up with you over lunch next week."

After work, Zarah walked up the rusted stairs to her apartment, planning to relax with X until Greg's shift ended. She sifted through her mail as she approached her door. Most were advertisements, but a crisp postcard with MONTANA written across a mountain-surrounded lake stood out from the rest. She flipped it over and read as she walked inside.

Zarah,

I'm so happy to hear about your therapy, your new job, and Greg. I would love to meet him one day. I'm also glad to hear that you're writing music with Behnam again. When you're ready, I would love to talk with you over the phone, or even over video (as you swear I can do with my computer). I miss you with my whole heart.

Love, Dad
P.S. - I'm proud of you.

Zarah knew her therapy might continue for several years. She knew that she would likely continue to have flashbacks and would have difficulty in crowds, especially with people she didn't know. She knew that the memory of the museum was still tightly packed away, but it was getting more organized as she wrote Z's story with Greg. "There is no known cure for PTSD," Katherine had told her earlier that week. "But rebuilding relationships—and building new ones—is important for your healing." Now inside her apartment, Zarah propped the postcard next to X's cage and handed him a sunflower seed.

Zarah's guitar rested on her bed, where she'd left it that morning. She picked it up and held it close to her body, feeling all the comfort of holding Scarlett but the familiarity of a hug from a lifelong friend. Energy filled her veins in the same way it did when she used to become Z, only she knew the feeling wasn't fleeting, wasn't something she needed to cling desperately to lest it slip away. She still had a long road ahead of her, but she'd found what she'd needed all along. It wasn't lightning or a mask or Greg or Behnam. It wasn't Z.

It was Zarah.

She began to strum.

The End

AUTHOR'S NOTE

On a Monday morning in 2013, I arrived a few minutes late to work, frustrated to miss my chance to grab tea before our morning meeting. Not long into that meeting, one of our co-workers (who had dialed in from a couple floors up) said he saw a man with a gun. We quickly secured our area, called emergency personnel, and sheltered in place for four hours. The things that we heard and saw that day were haunting.

Zarah's character is fictional, and while some of her symptoms may be representative of post-traumatic stress disorder (PTSD), each person experiences illness differently. Even having survived a mass shooting myself, I didn't think of myself as "someone with PTSD" until four years later, when I experienced my first flashback. It wasn't like a flashback in a movie—it was more like my imagination overtook me, overlaying details of that day onto the present and sending the same terror coursing through my body. And even then, I still didn't realize it was a flashback until I spoke with a friend of mine who also has PTSD.

If you or someone you know is experiencing symptoms of PTSD or other mental illness, there are outlets for help. If possible, you can seek the council of a licensed therapist. In addition, the below hotlines and websites are free resources:

- National Suicide Hotline: 1-800-SUICIDE (784-2433)
- National Suicide Prevention Lifeline: 1-800-273-TALK (8255)
- Safe Place: 1-888-290-7233
- National Alliance of the Mentally Ill: 1-800-950-6264
- The Trevor Project: 866-4-U-TREVOR
- National Sexual Assault Hotline: 800-656-HOPE

ACKNOWLEDGEMENTS

Many heartfelt thanks to all who read bits of this book, listened to me rant about it, and patiently nodded as I provided up-to-the-minute updates for an entire decade. In particular, thank you to Alaina, Paul, and Ginger from my writing group; Ben, Erin, and Kerrin, my beta readers; Swati Hegde my editor; J. L. Barnes my cover artist; and all who chose to remain anonymous for your invaluable patience, expertise, and advice.

Thank you to all of my teachers who encouraged my creativity, especially Frank Booth and Brad Barkley. To my students, for all you taught me. To my co-workers, especially those who were in the building with me, and those who help me navigate flashbacks from fire alarms now.

Thank you to my parents Brian and Mary for always encouraging me to dream big (I know you're reading in Heaven, Dad), and to my brothers Brian and Kevin who helped me believe I was awesome even when I was at my most awkward. Thank you to my enormous family of aunts, uncles, and cousins, and to my loving friends.

Thank you to my kiddos for lighting up my life. And thank you to my husband and partner Russell for answering my random questions about "hey what would you do if," listening to me plot and revise on long drives, looking at every potential character lookalike, and believing in me.

Finally, thank you to God (for like Greg, I was raised quite Catholic). My faith is central to who I am—even if a specific religion or creed is not—and without that faith, I never could have written this book.

The journey of writing this book has been emotional, liberating, and one of the great joys of my life. Thank you all—including those of you reading—for being a part of it.

ABOUT THE AUTHOR

Photo credit: Jo Russell Photography

Kate writes books about the people in her head, their quirks, their backstories, and their triumphs. By day, she writes about cloud computing. Otherwise, she's probably playing Dungeons and Dragons, painting impromptu murals, or having dance-offs with her kids.

Website: www.katewshea.com
Twitter: @katesheawrites
Facebook: www.facebook.com/katesheawrites